A Journey of a Lifetime

For the Women of
New Choices ___

In the "Spirit" of
A Journey of a Lifetime —

Peace —

William Carrusche

A JOURNEY OF A *L*IFETIME

A Novel

WILLIAM CARNUCHE

Author's Edition

William Carnuche

PPUBLISHING & COMPANY, INC.
PITTSBURGH
1995

PITTSBURGH

The above is a trademark of
Pittsburgh Publishing & Company, Inc.
4415 Fifth Avenue • Pittsburgh, PA 15213

ISBN: 0-9646225-0-5

Library of Congress Catalog Card Number: 95-68404

Book design by William Carnuche
Book jacket design by Rebecca A. McCaffrey,
    Barry J. Rudski and William Carnuche
Book jacket illustration by Rebecca A. McCaffrey
Book production by Barry J. Rudski
Book jacket photo by carl jacobitz

Printed in the United States of America
June 1995
First Edition

10 9 8 7 6 5 4 3 2 1

FOREWORD / APPRECIATION

The incidents and the characters in this novel are fictitious, purely the product of the writer's invention. I and my imagination assume all responsibility for the characters and actions portrayed in the book.

New Castle is a city in western Pennsylvania, the county seat of Lawrence County and situated at the confluence of the Beaver, Shenango, and Mahoning rivers, in an area where the Delaware, Huron, and various other Indians once roamed. It was founded in early 1798; John Calyle Stewart, from New Castle, Delaware, built the first cabin in the area, and later named the community in honor of his home town. The borough was made a city by decree on February 25, 1869.

During the early twentieth century, many historians referred to New Castle as "the tin capital of the world," and rightly so, since approximately 5,000 people of the community worked in the two tin mills of the city until the Carnegie-Illinois Steel Company closed them in 1937 and 1940.

I have taken the liberty of extending the life of the tin industry in New Castle to 1947, when the population of the city was about 48,500; presently (1990) the figure stands under 28,300. I also, with apologies to the citizens of New Castle and Mahoningtown, have placed all the Italian social clubs in the Mahoningtown area, when the majority were actually located on the south side of New Castle. I felt that the move was necessary to fit certain details in the action of the story.

The book you are about to read was written during the years 1972 through 1976 and revised in 1979 and 1994. I express my sincere appreciation to Montgomery Culver, Ph.D., of the writing program at the University of Pittsburgh, for his editing help during the various developmental stages of the book.

My thanks to Thomas F. McKeown for his great compassion for the grass roots movement of *A Journey of a Lifetime,* his legal advice and, most of all, his warm friendship. Thank you, Tom.

My unconditional love to the following friends for their

generous time in reading the book and their sincere encouragement: Suzy Adams, Ourania (Orrie) Beaven, Richard and Karen Cardosi, Anthony J. and Georgetta DeVasil-Carnuche, Teresa Ann Carnuche, Cheryl A. Braddick-Farren, William M. Hudgins, John L. Madden, Patricia L. Weber-McCaffrey, Gregg Page, Chris Rather, Christopher Ryan, Marlene Somar, Mark D. Spearman, Maria J. and Lena Marie Vello and Aurora R. Zamora. There are names unintentionally not listed who read the manuscript since 1976. You know who you are. I thank you.

Special thanks and my priceless gratitude to the following individuals for their generous extension of time and help in working with me on the January 15, 1995 New York Times Book Review advertisement: Harry M. DeWitt, Chairman, *Washington Star Newspaper Project*, Washington, D.C., Bob Hoover, Book Editor, *Pittsburgh Post-Gazette*, Pittsburgh, Mary Ann Lightfoot, MSW-LSW, Community Development Coordinator, Holy Family Institute of Pittsburgh, and John M. Wilds, Ph.D., Director, Human Resources, University of Pittsburgh, for their thoughtful comments on the book and their permission to use their quotations. Rebecca A. McCaffrey for her design and illustration of the characters. Barry J. Rudski, President, Magna Graphics, Inc., Pittsburgh, and production manager of the advertisement and Joseph G. Varvaro for his assistance. Leroy Baylor, Book Advertising Manager, *The New York Times Book Review,* for his assistance and words of wisdom concerning the post-Ad employ. Danny Baror, President, Baror International, Inc., Bedford, New York, for believing in the vision of the book, his encouragement and friendship. Alan G. Mason, President, The Gerald Company, P.C., Pittsburgh, for the strategic marketing plan, numerous recommendations and friendship. And, most important, Richard A. Bump, President, SMMS, Inc., Pittsburgh, for his support, his encouragement, and his warm, devoted friendship.

I am particularly grateful to the number of American individuals, book stores, universities, women's centers and shelters, CASA - "A child's voice in court" - The National Court

Appointed Special Advocate Association, Seattle, and my American and Canadian colleagues in the mental health profession who responded to the advertisement in wanting to read *A Journey of a Lifetime* as a tool in the continuing struggle against prejudice, battered women and children, the abandoned child and the disempowerment of women in America.

I am indebted to Tim Bailey, Executive Editor, Pittsburgh Publishing & Company, Inc., Pittsburgh, who "caught the vision" of *A Journey of a Lifetime*. Thank you, Tim, not only for being my editor and friend, but believing in the continuing struggle against domestic violence.

To all of the above people and organizations I owe so much; your thoughtful comments, your concern about societal problems and, most of all, your friendship.

Peace, W.C. 1995

For Giuseppina Vitelli and her
daughter, my mother Theresa Anne
Vitelli-Carnuche and her son,
my brother Joseph A. Carnuche
memoria in aeterna

and

With Unconditional Love:

For my family, especially the four
brothers from 13 Maintland Street—
Anthony, Joseph, William and John

and

For my friends — past and present

A Journey of a Lifetime

"When you teach your son,
you teach your son's son."

—*Talmud Kiddushin*

"The fathers have eaten sour
grapes, and the children's
teeth are set on edge."

—*Jeremiah 31:29*
The Old Testament

"The nature of a human being
is not to harm, but to help.

—*Buddha*

"Death and sorrow
will be the companions
of our journey; hardship
our garment..."

—*Sir Winston S. Churchill   1940*

PRELUDE

December 23, 1978

I

Only a handful of the older townspeople in the Western Pennsylvania mill town of New Castle still comment from time to time upon the violent end of the Samuel Di Santangelo family.

The only person who could tell the police much about the savage murder which took place on August 25th, 1947, was Miss Willie Hawkins, who timidly recounted to the officers the story of the fatal bludgeoning of Augustina Di Santangelo. Willie Hawkins, however, was entirely unwilling to talk to the newspaper reporters. When they questioned her about the killing or about the present whereabouts of the Di Santangelo children, her father, Dabney Hawkins, would step forward and say only that he and his daughter knew very little about the incident and that neither of them could say what had happened to Peter Di Santangelo and his sister, Connie.

"Were the children harmed in any way by Mr. Di Santangelo?" one of the pressman would invariably persist.

Typically, Dabney Hawkins would reply, "We don't know, sir. We don't know that happened except for what the police have already said to you, sir."

And, every now and then as the years went by, an ambitious journalism student or free-lance reporter would stop in the neighborhood to ask whether anything new was known of the two children or of their father, Mr. Samuel Di Santangelo. But, Dabney Hawkins would shake his head every time and say, "No, sir."

Peter Di Santangelo had indeed survived that hair-raising sundown of August 25th, 1947. But he had done so only because he had been able to banish the horrendous details of his family's tragic end to the most profound level of his subconscious. Miraculously, only an occasional stray thought related to that brutal evening managed to rise to the consciousness of Peter Di Santangelo from the depths to which it had been relegated.

On Friday evening, December 22nd, 1978, Peter was on assignment in Pittsburgh as a federal mediator in the contract negotiations between American Steel Industries Incorporated and the Associated Steel Workers.

Finally, the seven week strike which the workers had staged and which had been marked by occasional violence on the picket line, had been settled. Peter stepped out of the Soldier's and Sailor's Memorial Hall in the Oakland section of Pittsburgh where an emergency meeting had just ended. He paused for a moment on the terrace of the Memorial Hall and gazed out over the skyline. The mute winter sky was dull, grey and endless. Something tugged at his memory. He stood there for a few moments longer as though trying to force something to register in his mind; then he shook his head, dismissing whatever was nagging at him. He hurried down the steps and hailed a cab. "Please take me to the Hilton Hotel, sir," he directed the cabdriver quietly. He then asked the cabdriver how late the large department store next to the Hilton would be open that evening. He wanted to get another special gift for Margaret.

The following morning, Saturday, Peter walked up to the checkout counter at the Hilton and turned in his key. He was thirty-seven years old, six feet tall and the 197 pounds of weight he carried was solid. He was a handsome man, not in a classical way but rather his attractiveness was that of the rugged, hard-working, Mediterranean people he came from. His carriage, his manner and above all his way of looking directly at whomever he was addressing was so honest as to be slightly disarming. The combination was powerful and may have accounted to some extent for his success as a negotiator.

He smiled kindly at the woman behind the check-out counter at the Hilton as he handed her his room key. She returned his smile. "I hope that everything was satisfactory, sir," she said.

"Thank-you," said Peter, "Everything was more than satisfactory."

After he had finished checking out, he stepped to the Avis counter. He made arrangements for a rental car which he planned to drive to Erie and then to his home in Buffalo. "Could you tell me, please, which is the most direct route out of Pittsburgh to Erie?" he asked the Avis representative. She gave him a detailed route map. "And then Route 79 North will take you directly into Erie, Mr. Di Santangelo."

"Thank you," he said as he hurried away from the Avis counter and toward a telephone booth. He then telephoned his wife in Buffalo to tell her of his change of plans. "I'll be home this afternoon, Margaret. The strike is finally settled and I'm leaving Pittsburgh now. I have to make one stop in Erie to deliver a contract offer but I'll be home by four at the latest. Please give the children a hug for me. Good-bye, Margaret."

Peter, following the instructions he'd gotten from

the Avis clerk, reached Route I-79 easily. Picking up speed, he looked at his watch and knew that he had time for a leisurely drive home. He began to reminisce.

When he had left the orphanage in 1960, Peter enlisted in the Army, and after sixteen weeks of basic and advanced training at Fort Knox, he had been assigned orders to the 31st Transportation Battalion, stationed in Munich, Germany. He was sent to Fort Dix, New Jersey, for final preparations for the overseas flight.

On the Friday before the Monday morning flight, the enlisted personnel scheduled for foreign assignment were given weekend passes. Peter had never been to New York City. He had heard some people speak of it as an exciting, beautiful place, although others referred to the city as cold, grimy and offensive. Peter would have spent this last weekend with his family if he had had a family, but since the events of August, 1947, this was not the case. So, he hopped a bus at Fort Dix and headed for the "big city".

He stayed at the Biltmore Hotel, and after a full morning on a Manhattan tour bus, he rode another bus to the Bronx to see Yankee Stadium, where he allowed himself to think of his sister, Connie, and Mr. Dabney Hawkins.

He rode on to the uptown division of New York University to look at the bronze busts of great Americans who had been elected to the University's Hall of Fame. He then decided to return to the hotel to have dinner and to get ready for an evening in Times Square. He asked directions for taking the subway back to the neighborhood where his hotel was located, and at the 181st Street subway station he boarded the Broadway-Seventh Avenue Express. Peter sat next to a pleasant and attractive young woman who was as open as Peter was reserved. She had lovely, shiny brown hair which tossed as she spoke. Her smile was quick and her eyes whose color matched that of her hair seemed to smile even before the rest of her did.

But it was not that about the young woman's eyes which captured Peter's attention. It was that her eyes brought back a memory from long ago - a haunting memory of another woman's eyes which were as soft, brown and kind as were the eyes of this attractive woman.

Peter realized that his attention had been wandering as the young woman helped him to understand the peculiarities of the subway system of the city of New York.

Peter kept nodding his head to show her that he was understanding her. In the meantime, he noted that to his right sat a father, mother and two daughters of about twelve and fourteen who were dressed for a "family night out" at a movie or concert.

Three young black men, in their early twenties, got on the car at the Harlem stop, and because the seats were all taken, the blacks stood directly in front of Peter's bench, facing the white family on his right.

When the train pulled out of the station, one of the blacks fixed a direct stare on the older of the two white girls. As the Express rumbled on toward midtown, the black, holding onto the overhead grip, began leering at the girl and thrusting his crotch obscenely toward her. The action was conspicuous to the whole family and to everyone else on Peter's bench; riders on the other side of the car had been unaware of this situation until the horrified father jumped to his feet.

His mouth dropped open. He deliberately averted his eyes from the blacks then, swiftly, he lifted his terrified daughter bodily and placed her between himself and his horrified wife.

Grinning, the blacks immediately switched places so that the provocateur could continue to terrorize the child. The father jumped once again to his feet, then in a futile attempt to shield his whole family, he had no choice but to push himself between two of the blacks. The provocateur, with an infinitely slow sweeping gesture, slid a switch-blade knife from his pocket and sprang the blade free. The savage click of the blade against its handle, so quiet as to be nearly inaudible to the other passengers, thundered mightily in Peter's ears.

Seeing that a potentially violent scene was imminent, the other passengers collectively shrank toward the far end of the car. Peter was shocked into a state of immobility; a flashback to the terrible day in 1947 exploded instantly in his mind as he watched the black with the knife. He sat there, powerless to move from his seat. The young woman to his left sat motionless, watching carefully.

The tension broke as the train pulled into the Broadway 96th Street station in "white Manhattan" and the passengers jammed toward the exit doors in peak rush-hour fashion. The smirking blacks glided soundlessly in opposite directions toward different doors and melted into the platform crowds.

The family of four stumbled off the train, last to leave except for Peter, who trailed helplessly behind them and the woman who had remained calm throughout. As Peter mounted the stairs to the street, he glanced back and saw that the father was pouring out the story of what had just occurred to a policeman. The mother hugged her daughters tightly.

The young woman from the subway was speaking to Peter. He glanced at her but did not see her. He kept walking forward, all the while glancing over his shoulder at the policeman and the frightened family of four.

"Sir. Sir," the young woman repeated to Peter. "You're blocking the exit."

Peter moved hastily out of her way. As he reached the street level, still dazed, he followed the young woman. She looked back once at him, turned as though to walk forward, and then stopped and waited for him to reach her side.

"You really must not be so alarmed about what just happened on the subway," she said soothingly. "It's really very common."

"But I don't know what just happened on the subway. I only know that no one made a move to help that family back there. Not even me. I cannot believe that I just sat there and didn't lift a finger to help them." Peter seemed almost to be talking to himself.

"No, believe me. You did the right thing. It could have gotten really violent."

As they walked down the avenue together, Peter began to relax.

"I'm Margaret," said the brown-haired woman as she extended her hand to Peter. Shyly, Peter took her hand and shook it. Margaret guessed immediately that Peter, in his uniform, was from Fort Dix. And he was surprised to hear himself telling her freely of his assignment to Germany.

"I would think you are feeling lucky to be going to Germany. I'd love to go to Europe some day," said Margaret.

"Well," said Peter, "I don't know what to expect since I've never been there before."

"I have a roommate at Juilliard," said Margaret, "who studied in Paris before she came here, and she talks a great deal about the times she holidayed in Germany."

They spent the evening in Times Square, and on Sunday morning Margaret met Peter in the hotel lobby.

She took him on the Circle Line tour around the island of Manhattan. "This ride is about the corniest thing going on in New York, Peter, but it's still the best way to see the whole island."

Peter was happy to be in New York. He was doubly happy to be seeing this great city with such a lovely young woman.

When he happened to ask her what musical instrument she was concentrating upon, she answered, "Piano. I've studied it ever since I was a little girl in Jackson."

"Jackson where?"

"Jackson, Wyoming. I was born and raised there. Were you ever in Wyoming?"

"No. In fact, this is my first trip to New York. I haven't traveled at all until just recently in the Army. Isn't it awfully expensive to attend a school like Juilliard, not to mention living in a big city like New York?"

"I don't have to pay tuition; I auditioned for a scholarship and got lucky. I study with some of the best music instructors in the country."

"I think it's great you got the scholarship. You certainly must be proud of yourself." Peter hesitated. He cleared his throat. "Your parents must be very proud of you," he said. Peter wondered why he had hesitated before he had said that. It was very hard for Peter to talk about parents given his own bittersweet background.

"Proud of myself?" asked Margaret. "Because I go to

Juilliard? I've been studying the piano ever since I was a very little girl."

"Well, I'll bet a lot of others did too, and didn't make it. I would be proud to say I went to Juilliard if I were in music."

"You never studied an instrument?"

"I can't even whistle."

"Well, the only thing I can tell you is it's a lot of work."

"What? Learning to whistle?"

Margaret laughed. "Yes, learning to whistle. I meant the training at the school."

After the Circle Line tour, they spent the rest of the day walking in Central Park. They laughed together. They had fun together and that was the thing that mattered most to Peter. He loved the fun that he and Margaret shared on that innocent day of their second meeting. It had been a long, long time since Peter Di Santangelo had laughed so fully and so freely. In fact, had he ever? Something flashed into his mind. Some memory which he couldn't quite grasp. And, typically, as quickly as that half-memory flashed into his mind, it flickered for only a moment and was gone.

Just one hour before Peter's bus was scheduled to depart for Fort Dix, they strolled into the Biltmore lobby. They stopped near the front desk, and stood facing one another.

"I am so very happy to have met you, Margaret; the

day's been just great."

"I'm happy too, Peter, to have met you and to have spent the day with you. I've loved being your guide." Margaret, smiling, took out a pen and a slip of paper from her purse and began to write. "Here's my address at school. If you want to write, I promise to write back."

Peter took the paper and put it in the pocket of his uniform shirt. He smiled. "Thank you, Margaret. As soon as I get settled on base in Munich, Germany, I'll write." Margaret looked tenderly at Peter. He smiled at her then quickly looked away.

They parted and went their separate ways. On the bus back to Fort Dix, Peter thought about the hours they had just spent together. "It was the fun we had that I loved most," he murmured to the reflection of himself in the bus window. Deliberately, he did not think about her soft, brown eyes. Peter closed his eyes and leaned his head against the seat's head rest. He thought quietly about his weekend with Margaret.

They corresponded for three years. One night when Peter was in the Munich's Hofbrauhaus, he bought a post card. He wrote to her, 'Margaret. I love you. Peter.' She returned the same post card, reversing the names, posted a new airmail stamp over the original one, and readdressed the card to Munich.

During the seasons of their letter writing, and even after they were married, Peter never mentioned the violence that had taken place in his childhood. Margaret knew little of the origins of Peter Di Santangelo; only that he had been born in New Castle and began his schooling in the orphanage.

Midway in his tour in Germany, Peter wrote Margaret that he had saved enough money and leave time to come to New York at Christmas to see her. She replied that she planned to go home to Jackson for Christmas, and that the winters there were bitter cold and inhospitable to newcomers; she went on to say that she always loved her visits home during the month of August, the summer break from the conservatory. Peter understood, and in August of 1962 he flew from Germany to Wyoming to be with Margaret and to meet her family. For the first time since 1947 he sat at a table with a family, and for the first time in his life enjoyed a family in which the father sat down with the wife and child to talk, laugh, give compliments, show affection and respect.

Every person dreams of finding their Walden Pond. Many search a lifetime and are unable to complete the heartbeat journey to this dream. Peter found it in Jackson, Wyoming.

Jackson is the southern entrance to the Grand Tetons National Park. With Margaret and her mother and father, he visited the Shoshone and Arapaho villages on the Wind River Reservation near the city of Lander. And as they drove in Yellowstone National Park, where Peter saw his first brown bear, deer, moose, elk, and antelope, Margaret repeatedly asked her father to stop the jeep so that she could show Peter the Indian paintbrush, with its small green stalk surrounded by bright red leaves.

The family took him to a championship rodeo, where Margaret's screams and yells startled him; but her father assured him that she would be fine and that he should just enjoy the spectacle.

Peter fell in love with the Lord's creation of the Grand Tetons, Peter's Walden Pond, not only because of the majesty and glory of the landscape, God's image of tranquility, but because here Margaret had spent her childhood and had grown. And it was a place where Peter was able to forget what had happened to his own family. He told Margaret's father how much he loved Margaret and how much he hoped to return to Jackson and someday with the parents' blessing, to marry their daughter.

When his enlistment was up, Peter returned to Philadelphia in 1963 and started night school at the University of Pennsylvania, and he made his annual trips to Jackson to be with Margaret and her family. He graduated six years later and accepted a federal government position in the Department of Labor. In the summer of 1969, in Jackson, he and Margaret were married. She came east with him to Buffalo, where he was assigned to the district office of the Labor Department.

II

A directional sign on Route 79 North shot a sudden charge of agitation through Peter's mind. He wasn't quite sure that he had read it correctly. Involuntarily, his right foot hit the brake pedal. Voluntarily, he slid it back onto the accelerator. The sign read:

New Castle Exit
2 Miles

Something grabbed at his throat. He found it hard to swallow. Somewhere in his mind he heard the sound of a blow being struck - something cracked. He slammed his foot hard against the accelerator. He was just beginning to compose himself when he saw a second directional signal which read:

New Castle Exit
1 Mile

Peter tightened up. He forced himself to sit upright in the seat. His heart was thumping. He could not swallow. From a distant echo in his mind, the command rang out, "Run, Peter, Run!" A third directional sign appeared:

New Castle Exit

Peter tightened up all over; his nerves tingled harshly. The huge exit sign loomed up and suddenly without making any real decision, he swung the Avis car onto the exit ramp and soon found himself circling onto a state road toward New Castle, the town where he had been born and spent the first six years of his life.

At the edge of the city he pulled into a service station and asked the young attendant for directions to the viaduct.

"The what, sir?"

"The viaduct that leads to the tin mill," replied Peter.

The boy's puzzled frown deepened. "The tin mill?" He gaped at Peter. "Are you sure you're in the right city, mister?"

"Yes, I'm in the right city. Is your manager here, or somebody older?"

The boy beckoned to a large man in his late forties

with grease on his clothes, face and hands. He too responded with a quizzical look. "Viaduct? Tin mill? There's no tin mill in this neck of the woods." He paused, then asked, "Where 'bouts you tryin' to get to in New Castle?"

"To be honest with you, I don't exactly know. It was a long time ago. There was a bridge in the city, and at the end of the bridge was the tin mill. It was over in the area where the black people lived, at that time anyway."

The manager's face took on a brighter expression. "I bet you're talkin' about the steel mill over past Moravia Street hill." He smiled. "You want the steel mill, not the tin mill. No tin mill around this city. And those colored people you talked about, they still live over there, but it's a housing project now. The steel mill sits right across the street from the housing project. I'll tell you the easiest way there. Are you familiar with New Castle at all?"

"No, sir. It's been too long for me to remember anything at all about this city."

Peter found the man's directions easy to follow. In a few minutes he was going down Lutton Street, and then he turned south on Moravia Street. He could just see the top of the viaduct as he followed the route.

A large discount hardware store stood on the left of the entrance to the viaduct. Peter pulled into the store's parking lot and faced the bridge. He sat back. His memory and imagination crossed back and forth, searching with sharp, piercing concentration. He could not see the other end of the viaduct because of the drop in the arch at the other end of the bridge; all he could see was the roof of the big mill and a large multistory building in the housing project which had not existed in 1947.

And then Peter's mind, struck with an amazement of terror, started to call back an awareness of his childhood years in this city from which he had been so violently wrenched from his family.

"Mother is the name of God
in the lips and hearts of little
children."

—*William Makepeace Thackeray 1848*

"Loneliness and the feeling of
being unwanted is the most
terrible poverty."

—*Mother Teresa 1975*

PATHETIQUE

SUMMER 1947

I

On June 25, 1947, Peter Di Santangelo celebrated his sixth birthday, and the first anniversary of his knowledge that his mother's first name was Augustina, not "Whore."

Peter who lived with his father, mother, sister and maternal grandmother was average in height for his young, six years. His dark brown hair was "stick straight" except where an occasional cowlick caused it to poke into the air unnecessarily. Mostly, Peter was a gentle, serious and watchful child. Now and then, when something really tickled him, a grin would light his hazel-green eyes and his little face so dramatically that for those few moments, it was almost impossible to recall the serious little boy he was most of the time.

Peter's family lived in the black district of New Castle, Pennsylvania. To the east of the neighborhood was the viaduct, the dividing line which separated the black district from the white people of New Castle. At the west end of the neighborhood stood the New Castle Tin Mill Corporation, and beyond the mill was the predominantly Italian village of Mahoningtown, a borough generally called "Little Italy."

Mr. Samuel Di Santangelo, Peter's father, who worked at the tin mill, drank too much. Every Friday evening, after he was paid, he would leave the mill and head straight for Mahoningtown where during the coarse of the evening, he would wander from the Sons of Italy to the Casa Savoia. By the time he staggered drunkenly into the King Humbert Hall on Sunday night, the foolishness and anger which had been steadily building during the weekend would have become nothing short of insanity and rage.

Peter's mother and grandmother did their best to provide a home for the family. Augustina, his mother, and, when school was not in session, his sister Connie, would fill a large two-handled basket with fresh-baked bread, pizza slices, and Mother's Oats oatmeal cookies. Mother and daughter would then carry them to the tin mill to sell during the noon hour. They would return to the mill at three o'clock and again at seven-fifteen in the evening during the second shift's lunch break. Peter's grandmother, Mrs. Vitello, was blind. The delicate love which Peter felt for his grandmother could be seen in the many things he did for her daily without complaint. It was especially so when he spoke her name, Mamo.

Mamo made the family's clothes which was for Connie an endless source of embarrassment and discomfort.

"I refuse to wear any more of these dumb dresses, Mom!" she would screech in the high-pitched tones of an anguished adolescent. "The kids laugh at me, Mom. I feel ridiculous!"

"Connie, please," Augustina would reply over and over again. "Don't let Mamo hear you complaining. Your dresses are fine, honey. You know perfectly well that I only buy Gold Medal flour, which costs a good dime more because we know that the colored prints on the sacks are the best to be had. I think Mamo does a wonderful job on all of our clothes."

"But why does Mamo have to make them at all? Nothing ever fits!"

Augustina sighed aloud, her tiredness showing. She pushed a stray lock of hair away from her forehead and wiped her hand on her flowered apron. She looked intently at her daughter, her eyes begging for Connie to understand.

"Please, Connie, no more fuss! You know that I cannot afford the time or the money to buy your dresses.

She tried to put her arm around her daughter but Connie shied away contemptuously.

"But I'm ashamed, Mom!" Connie would whine.

"Ashamed of what, Connie? Your clothes are fine and I don't understand why you make such a fuss over the everyday dresses you wear to school. Now that's enough!"

Augustina walked to the round kitchen table and placed a basket of fresh, sweet-smelling homemade bread in the center of it. "I would think you'd be used to the school kids by now. You better just adjust to paying no mind to your schoolmates."

"I'll adjust to hitting Patty Ann Johnson right in her damn mouth—", shouted Connie.

"Here! Here!" Augustina interrupted, frowning at her daughter. "What did I tell you about that language of yours? Can't you talk about anything without cussing, Connie?"

Peter's sister would plead, whine and insist but nothing changed.

"I simply cannot afford to buy your dresses, Connie, and I have nothing more to say on the subject."

After she had made her final statement, Augustina walked to the stove and stirred the tomato sauce, as though symbolically she had moved into a realm which had nothing to do with Connie's dresses. Eventually, Connie would give up trying to convince her mother and sulk off to her room.

Connie was a pretty child or could have been if her face had not been so consistently distorted by the anger which was becoming more and more ingrained in her. Unlike Peter, she was tall for her age but like him she had lovely, hazel-green eyes. But, she was so different from him in so many ways that except for the physical resemblance they bore to one another, it was hard to recognize that they were brother and sister.

Whereas Connie lived in a state of constant embarrassment and turmoil, Peter was mostly peaceful and accepting.

He was never embarrassed because the buttons did not match the buttonholes on his shirts. He was too young to understand proper appearance, as were Peter's young, black playmates in the neighborhood. It didn't matter to them or to Peter what anyone wore. These children's days were guided by one critical question: Who would be the good guys and who the bad in their daily cap-gun battles? These were the things that really mattered to Peter and as he listened to Connie's daily, sometimes hourly whining to Augustina, he did not understand any of it. He would sit with his chin propped on his hands listening, listening to the two of them, his silent gaze moving back and forth from his mother to his sister but try as he might he did not understand what they were fighting about.

Augustina and their grandmother took Peter and Connie to the Salvation Army Headquarters every other

Saturday morning to see Mrs. Major Hoffman who was head of the general aid section.

Mrs. Major Hoffman tried her best to help the Di Santangelo family. She knew of their problem with Mr. Di Santangelo and had once visited their home at a time when Augustina had assured her that her husband would be at home. Mrs. Major Hoffman had planned to talk to him about the disastrous effect his drinking was having on his family.

When she arrived that day, Augustina greeted her at the door and showed her into the family's parlor. Mr. Di Santangelo sat at the farthest end of the room.

"Mr. Di Santangelo," said Mrs. Major Hoffman in a quiet voice. "Are you aware of how much damage you are doing to your poor wife and children because of your terrible drinking habit?"

He turned his attention to Mrs. Major Hoffman. "If I had my way," he said glaring at her, "I would see to it that all you sons 'a bitches were locked up as trouble-makers!"

"But you must realize the terrible effect you are having on your whole family, Mr. Di Santangelo," she said. "Your wife is losing control over your eleven-year-old daughter, and you cannot expect your mother-in-law to continue walking to the farm. We have an excellent program at the Headquarters which can help you overcome your drinking problem, Mr. Di Santangelo, but you must be willing to come into the program so that we will be able to—"

"I don't give a fuck what you have at that goddamn whorehouse!" yelled Mr. Di Santangelo. "Just get the hell out of here and leave my family alone!" He then turned to Augustina and said, "Don't ever let me hear about you going back to that fucking place again. If you do, Whore, I'll kill you, and tear that fucking place down!"

"Please, Sam," Augustina begged. Her voice quivered as she tried valiantly to control herself. "Just listen to what Mrs. Major Hoffman is saying. I'll go with you to the meetings, Sam. Please, Sam, if you quit drinking, everything will be all right again. I know it will, Sam. Please just listen to her, Sam," she said.

"And the whoring, bitch? Does the program stop the fucking whoring?"

"Sam! My God you know that's not true. And in front of the children! It's the drinking that brings out that evil kind of talk. You never acted like this until you took to drinking every night, Sam."

"Did you hear me ask about the whoring, bitch?" He pointed to the Major as he yelled at Augustina. "Get her the fuck out of this house right now! And once again, whore, if you ever go back to that whorehouse again, I'll kill you. Do you understand me? Go back to the Salvation Army and you're one dead bitch!"

But, Augustina and her family continued their bi-weekly visits to the Army headquarters. When Connie or Peter had a problem, their mother encouraged them to ask the Major for advice. If the grandmother had questions, Augustina would ask the Major in English then repeat to Mrs. Vitello in Italian, the Major's suggestions.

On one visit, Connie presented one of her many problems at school: Patty Ann Johnson had called her a "white nigger" because her family lived in the black district of the city and Connie wanted to know if it was okay "to hit the goddamn bitch in the mouth."

Mrs. Major Hoffman sat at her roll-top desk; its flexible top of narrow tin and wooden strips was pushed back, revealing a monumental pile of papers, public records and memoranda.

"Connie, hitting someone for saying things we don't like to hear will not make the problem go away. What you have to do is ignore the girl and not trouble yourself over anything she says to you." She reached out and took Connie's slender hand in her own. She smiled at the troubled youngster and spoke. "And, Connie, you should try not to use that kind of language when you're talking about people. It isn't any different from what that girl said to you. When you hear people use a vulgar or unkind word about another person, such as the colored people or poor white people or anyone else, just pray for that person's soul. Do you understand me, Connie?"

"Yes, Major, I understand you but she upsets me so much!"

"Yes, Connie, I know she does. But you have to re-member what I said to you. Pray for the person who upsets you."

Peter was sitting quietly listening to all that Mrs. Major Hoffman had said to his sister. He leaned for-ward in his chair and called softly to Mrs. Major Hoffman that he knew only one prayer, the one he said at night before he went to bed.

"Of course, Peter," said Mrs. Major Hoffman kindly. "It is quite proper for you to say your prayer, Peter, any time you feel it is necessary to ask the Lord to save a soul."

Peter remembered her advice, and later, during his school years at the orphanage, upon hearing someone say "nigger," he immediately said:

> *"Now I lay me down to sleep,*
> *I pray the Lord my soul to keep,*
> *If I should die before I wake,*
> *I pray the Lord my soul to take."*

Mrs. Major Hoffman turned to Connie, "Now you go over and sit with your grandmother. I want to talk with your mother."

Augustina stood up, walked over to the desk and sat down in the large wooden chair previously occu-pied by her daughter.

"Hello, Mrs. Major."

"Hello, Augustina." The Major handed Augustina a form. "Here is the seven-dollar certificate. Give it to the store manager at the A & P store on Mill Street for his initials; then you can redeem it for food.

Augustina put the certificate in her purse. The Major studied her and then put a hand on her arm. "Augustina, I see where your husband hit you again." She looked up at Peter, then faced Augustina again. "And I see that Peter has a bandage on the back of his head. Did his father hit him again?"

"Yes," replied Augustina, keeping her eyes on the bruise on her arm. "I don't know what I'm going to do with Sam, Mrs. Major Hoffman. He would kill me if he knew I was sitting here talking to you this very minute."

"Yes, I know. I'm frightened for you and your son. But Mr. Di Santangelo doesn't permit me to visit you, so I have to depend on you, Augustina, to convince him of the importance of attending our program."

Augustina raised her soft brown eyes and looked sadly at Mrs. Major Hoffman. She put a quivering hand to her face and then began to cry. "I'm so tired, Mrs. Major Hoffman. I'm so tired."

Peter stretched his feet to the ground and slipped off of the chair on which he had been sitting. He walked over to his mother, put his arms around her and kissed her.

II

Most days during the spring and summer, Peter walked with his grandmother to Mr. Bump's farm, about four miles southeast of New Castle, near a hamlet called West Pittsburg, without the h, in the Wampum area. After Peter had eaten his oatmeal, they would leave the house at five o'clock in the morning and walk to the farm.

The countryside surrounding New Castle was especially wonderful in those quiet, early morning hours. It was a special time for Peter and his grandmother. Mrs. Vitello would tell her grandson about her home town in Italy, Baia 'E Latina, a small village near Caserta, north of Naples. Guiseppina Ragosta had been born in May of 1879 and had married Giuseppi Vitello on January 14, 1894, in Baia 'E Latina. Peter's grandfather had come to the United States in 1891, and after working for a year with the Lake Erie Railroad, he had ventured to visit a friend from his home town who had settled near Pittsburgh. They journeyed to New Castle to visit a relative of the friend, and Giuseppe learned of the heavy demand for immigrants to work in the New Castle tin mills.

He worked there for two years in order to save enough money to return to Baia 'E Latino to marry Giuseppina. After a long cart ride from their home town, they emigrated to the United States from Naples, and arrived in New York on January 25, 1894, on the German vessel Kaiser.

Four months short of Mrs. Vitello's fifteenth birthday, they settled in New Castle, and were never able to return to Italy to visit their families. Peter's grandfather had died in 1925 while at work in the tin mill, and although Peter had never known him, Mrs. Vitello spoke so warmly of him and told such stories about him that Peter grew to love him very much.

Mrs. Vitello would sing Italian songs as they walked along Route 168 to the farm. She always wore a long black sweater over the even longer black dress which covered her black stockings. She pinned a white apron to the front of her dress with two safety pins; one held the top of a large crucifix, and the other held a medal of St. Anthony, a medal of St. Joseph, another of St. John, and her most treasured of all, a medal of St. Theresa. Her thick white hair, tied in a knot at the back of her head, always reminded Peter of the color of newly fallen snow.

She walked with a white cane, given to her by Mrs. Major Hoffman in one hand, while the other rested on Peter's shoulder. Midway through their journey, she would take out her large rosary beads and recite the Hail Mary four times. Peter was always expected to answer the "Amen" at the end of each prayer, and, if he got bored or distracted by looking out for an Indian or a pirate, Mrs. Vitello would whack him on top of his head with her cane, restoring to him the proper respect due to the Lord's Mother. "Amen! Amen! Amen!"

They would arrive at Mr. Bump's farm at about eight o'clock, and Peter would leave his grandmother standing by the vegetable plants while he went into the farmhouse to register Mrs. Vitello with an "X." He would return to his grandmother with the baskets and then direct her hands at the picking of beans, tomatoes or radishes, while she entertained the rest of the work crew with her Italian songs. They received four dollars plus a large bag of green beans to take home with them when they left at three o'clock each afternoon. And on their way home, Peter heard the same stories about his grandfather, about the Volturno River and Baia 'E Latina, listened to the same songs and recited the same "Amens" four more times around the rosary; he received an occasional whack on his head from the cane because he felt sure he had seen Geronimo hiding in one of the bushes along Route 168.

On a Friday, shortly after Peter's sixth birthday, when he and his grandmother arrived home from their day at the farm, his mother was in the kitchen preparing supper. She had on her blue dress with white polka dots, the dress which, it seemed to Peter, she always wore. She never wore makeup, and her hair, although not the color of snow, was always tied in a knot at the back of her head, just like Mrs. Vitello's. Augustina kissed her mother, then hugged Peter and asked him, "Did my big boy take care of Mamo today?" As always, Peter replied, "Yes, Mom."

Augustina, removing her mother's black sweater, said to Peter, "Take Mamo up to the bathroom and help her wash up, honey. And make sure she lies down till supper." She laid her hand on Peter's head. "If you're not too tired, you wash up and come back down and help mom in the kitchen."

After helping his grandmother wash and dry her face and hands, Peter guided her into the bedroom that they shared with Connie, who was fully stretched out on her bed. Peter walked Mrs. Vitello over to their bed and guided her head to the pillow. He lifted her legs, invisible under her long black dress, to the foot of the bed, and started to unlace her shoes.

"And don't make any goddamn noise, either," Connie said. "I'm sleeping."

"You can't be sleeping, Sister, if you're talking," Peter said, looking at Connie with a slight smile on his face.

"Are you getting smart with me, you little turd? And close that goddamn door!"

"Wait until I'm done with Mamo." Peter took off Mrs. Vitello's old-fashioned black tie shoes and put them under the bed. He laid her precious medals on top of the dresser, then returned to the bed, leaned over to kiss his grandmother, and headed for the door.

Connie put her hands behind her head as she watched him. "Now don't forget to tell Mom I called you a little turd, shit-head."

Peter ignored her, closed the door, and headed downstairs to the kitchen.

"Why is Sister in bed?" he asked his mother.

"Miss Willie caught her and the Hunter boy smoking in the Thompson's garage today. I don't know what I'm going to do with that sister of yours, Peter." Augustina was stirring tomato sauce in a large metal pot. "How a girl of eleven years old, just going into sixth grade, can be so bad, I just don't know."

"The Mrs. Major said that she won't act that way when she gets older."

Augustina lifted the wooden spoon from the pot and tasted the sauce. She reached for the salt box and shook it over the pot, then stirred some more. "I sure hope Mrs. Major Hoffman knows what she's talking about, honey. If I could only get Connie to stop cussing, maybe the smoking and hitting other children would go away. I hope the good Lord sees His way of changing that girl once she gets to junior high school.

She tasted the sauce again and put the spoon on a saucer on top of the stove. "Looks as if we'll have some extra sauce for a side dish, Peter. How about taking those green beans over to the sink? You can clean them for me; we'll put some sauce on them and have them along with the pasta. She filled another large kettle midway with water and carried it to the table. "Come here, Peter. It'll be easier here than at that sink." She lifted Peter and set him on the table. "You be careful with the piercer, because I don't want to have to take you to the hospital. Wait until I get a newspaper for you."

She took a newspaper from a cupboard drawer and spread it on the table between Peter and the kettle. "Now, you mind about this piercer. And don't get the bag wet; you and Mamo will need it when you go to the farm Monday."

Peter started to cut the ends off the green beans, dropping each end onto the paper and each bean into the kettle of water.

Augustina always watched out for her son's safety. When her husband came home drunk, she always made sure that Peter was out of his sight, usually she sent him over to Miss Willie Hawkins.

Mr. Di Santangelo's usual response to Peter's presence was the accusation that the boy was not his child. Although Peter did not understand the full implication of this charge until later in life, at the orphanage, he did understand his mother's instructions never to go near his father and, when outdoors, never to answer his call.

One afternoon a few months earlier, Peter, playing in the yard, had not known that his father was in the neighborhood until he realized that Mr. Di Santangelo was standing next to him. He was overcome with terror and could not budge. His father grabbed him but Peter somehow broke the hold and started to run toward the Shenango River in back of the house.

Peter was always able to outrun his father because of Mr. Di Santangelo's drunkenness. And he always ran for the river bank behind their house next to the tin mill where he would hide among the tin mill shipping cargo crates stacked near the river and the railroad tracks.

His father shouted and called him indecent names during the fruitless pursuit. Peter, in his terror, stumbled over a rock and fell to his knees. His father snatched up the nearest stone, threw it at his son and caught him squarely on the back of his head. Peter tottered to his feet and holding his hand to the bleeding wound made it to the cargo crates where he waited, crying and trembling in fear, for his mother. After some time, Augustina found him there hiding behind a wooden crate. She took him, his hair matted with blood, to the hospital where five sutures where required. Peter spent the night at Miss Willie and Mr. Dabney Hawkins' house.

After Peter finished cutting the green beans, Augustina inspected the kettle. "Miss Willie and Mr. Hawkins are coming over for supper tonight, honey," she said.

III

Willie Hawkins, the Di Santangelos' next-door neighbor, was a black woman who kept house for her father, Dabney Hawkins, a retired peanut picker from Suffolk, Virginia. Miss Willie had explained in the neighborhood that she and her father had come to town because Mr. Hawkins had heard back in Suffolk that his younger stepbrother, Timothy Mellon, who had left Suffolk some years earlier, was said to be living in New Castle. Willie Hawkins said that when she and Mr. Hawkins had arrived in the city, right after the war, it seemed that no one in the neighborhood had heard of Mr. Timothy Mellon and family. But finally Mr. Butler

Frank Brinker, whose mother had named him after her home town, Butler, Pennsylvania, had told Miss Willie that a gentleman by the name of Mellon had come to the area back in the late Thirties, along with his wife and four daughters, and had worked in the tin mill for three years; he had by then headed for Detroit, with two other families from the neighborhood, to work in the automobile plants.

Mr. Butler Frank Brinker didn't know whether the name had been Timothy Mellon, since the family had kept mainly to itself, but thought that his wife Mrs. Brinker had known the full name; she, however, had died four years past.

But Willie Hawkins had later heard at Mr. Tom's general store that the wife of the vanished Mellons had told Mr. Tom's wife, Miss Libby, that the family was headed for Mobile, Alabama. Mr. Tom told Willie Hawkins that the store account had been registered to a Mr. T. Mellon, and that he, Mr. Tom, had sent off a letter to his second cousin in Hattiesburg, Mississippi, about ninety-six miles west of Mobile, instructing the cousin to try to locate Mr. T. Mellon in order to collect the eight dollars and eighteen cents the family still owed Mr. Tom for food supplies on the account.

As it turned out, Dabney Hawkins decided that he and his daughter were not about to head for Detroit, Mobile or anywhere else to look for a younger step-brother whom he had not seen since 1937. They settled in New Castle, where Miss Willie took in laundry and did housecleaning, while her father worked as a groundskeeper on the FitzSimons estate in the North Hill section of the city.

Willie Hawkins had a strong craving for spaghetti, and when Augustina could muster two extra plates of pasta, she would invite the Hawkins over for supper.

When they arrived that evening, Willie Hawkins was wearing a white service uniform and a blue and white handkerchief knotted at the back of her head; her father was still wearing his green cotton work shirt and trousers and black high-topped work shoes. The laces were untied and caught under his soles as he walked into the house.

When supper was almost ready, Augustina sent Peter upstairs to fetch Mrs. Vitello and Connie. When they arrived downstairs, Miss Willie and Dabney Hawkins were already seated at the kitchen table.

"Lord, Miss Augustina!" Willie Hawkins exclaimed, "I've had my mouth set all day on spaghetti, and the good Lord Himself knows there isn't anyone in this neighborhood excepting Miss Augustina to make the best spaghetti I have ever eaten."

"Well, you can eat all the spaghetti you want, Miss Willie," said Augustina. And smiling warmly at her friend she placed a large bowl of piping hot tomato sauce on the table.

"Mr. Tom's been mighty good to us. Just yesterday

he gave us a twenty-five-pound sack of flour for only a dollar twenty, and you know what flour sells for these days." She carried the pasta kettle over to the sink and poured the contents into a colander. "And last week, Mr. Tom's wife, Miss Libby, gave me five empty sacks with the prettiest colored prints you'd ever want to see for making clothes."

"Miss Libby is a kind soul, Miss Augustina, although she does tend to run a lot at the mouth to the shoppers. But none the less, you can count on Miss Libby's help when she can help others."

Augustina placed the bowl of drained spaghetti on the table next to the bread. She sat down and asked Dabney Hawkins to say the grace.

Dabney Hawkins lowered his head. "O Lord, we thy people and sheep of thy pasture, we give thee thanks for this table before thy people. And blessed is he that considereth the poor, for the Lord will deliver him in time of trouble. Amen."

The news about the new colored print bags had not pleased Connie who made a face.

"If Mr. Tom gave us anything cheap," she said, "you can bet there's something wrong with it, and you can also bet we're eating flour worms with our spaghetti if he and Miss Libby gave us flour cheap."

"There that girl goes again!" remarked Willie Hawkins. "How that child of yours talks, Miss Augustina! And washing her mouth out with soap and water is just wasting a good bar of soap. Just the day before last, that girl came running through my back yard chasing the young Taylor boy and the Lord knows that boy is two times as small as that girl of yours, and I don't have the mouth to repeat where that child said she was going to kick that poor boy when she caught him!"

"Connie!" Augustina said sharply. "You just stop that kind of talk right now! If you can't talk civilized in front of people, then you don't belong in front of people. And you're certainly not impressing any of us with your swearing. Don't you ever listen to anything Mrs. Major Hoffman tells you?"

"I'm not about to pay her any mind, Mom," answered Connie. "Do you know what Mrs. Major said to me when we were over at the schoolyard playing baseball yesterday? She came by the schoolyard all decked out in that silly Army outfit of hers, and right in front of all my friends—"

"Friends?" Willie Hawkins interrupted. "And since when has anyone, excepting that evil Hunter boy, taken to you as a friend?"

Connie looked at Willie Hawkins and then turned back toward her mother. "As I was saying before the cry of the old crow, right there in front of my friends, Mrs. Major Hoffman started asking me all sorts of stupid questions about the way I was behaving in the schoolyard and at home too."

"You're calling those stupid questions?" Willie Hawkins said. "I don't know about your feelings, Miss Augustina, but it sure seems to me that the Mrs. Major sure knows this girl." To Connie she said, "What's this I hear about you stealing the ball from the other kids and running into the woods with it? You hid that ball from the other kids so they couldn't play baseball!"

"You're crazy!" Connie replied.

"I'm crazy?" Miss Willie pointed a finger at herself. "Tell this woman you were not hiding in those woods, and every time someone hit that ball near the end of the schoolyard, you didn't come out of those woods, grab that ball and ran and hid!"

"I don't know what you're talking about!" Connie turned to her mother. "Anyway, the Mrs. Major asked me if I got into trouble with the playground guard by cussing and things like that. She really burns me up, Mom! Even my friend Jimmy Bobjack Hunter told me he thought the Mrs. Major walks like she has a broom handle caught up her you know what!"

"Connie!" yelled Augustina.

"I'm just repeating what Jimmy Bobjack said, Mom."

"Smack that child, Miss Augustina!" Willie Hawkins demanded. "Lord if she doesn't sound like Mr. Sam with that mouth of hers!"

Dabney Hawkins had been talking quietly with Peter about baseball. He lifted his head, looked at Connie, and then said to his daughter, "I think you better hush up a little, Miss Willie. You and that girl are both a little hardheaded, and you don't have any right to talk about Mr. Sam like that, especially in front of his family. Your mother taught you a long time ago what a guest is in another person's home. Now suppose we eat our food and let Mr. Sam be for the time being."

Willie Hawkins frowned at her father. "I don't think you should tell this woman to hush up, Mr. Hawkins. Not after what I have gone through with you this day."

"What the hell happened, Mr. Hawkins?" inquired Connie staring right into his face.

"I think you'd better go up to your room for the rest of the evening, Connie," said Augustina. "I have had it with that mouth of yours, and I am not going to put up with it any more. Do you hear me? I am not going to ask you again to mind your language."

"All I asked, Mom, was what happened today that got..." She nodded toward Willie Hawkins, "You know who so upset?"

"Don't go nodding your head at me, girl! And you mind what your mother has said to you!"

Connie looked at Willie Hawkins. "I am asking Mr. Hawkins a question, not you! And why did you tell my mother that I was smoking in old man Thompson's garage today? I wasn't anywhere near his place today. And whatever gave you the idea I smoke in the first place?"

"Don't you ever, young girl, call this woman a liar!"

Willie Hawkins replied. "There isn't anyone in this neighborhood can come up with the cock-and-bull fish stories that come out of your mouth! And I have never in my life heard things coming out of the mouths of grown-ups excepting Mr. Sam, the words I hear coming out of your mouth!" She turned abruptly to her father. "I told you before, and before that, Mr. Hawkins, not to go into the white folks' drinking gardens. Someday you are going to get killed by those people! Walking into those places bigger than the statue this city put up in Diamond Square!"

"I don't care what you have to say about that, Miss Willie," Dabney Hawkins told his daughter without looking at her. "Your father walked clear across town on this hot day and now you sit there and tell me I am not to go in a saloon for one glass of beer, with the money in my pocket to pay for it?" He looked up at Augustina. "That man tried to tell me he wasn't going to serve me a glass of beer because I was drunk, Miss Augustina, and I only had one bottle of beer all day, and that was this morning before I went to work at the FitzSimons."

"You don't seem to understand what I mean, Mr. Hawkins," Willie Hawkins said. "You just don't belong in those beer gardens in the first place. You can stop here in the neighborhood at Mr. Adams' saloon, or you can come right home. You know this woman always makes sure you have beer in the house. There just isn't any sense to you walking into those white people's beer gardens unless you are looking for trouble. And if it is the trouble you're looking for, Mr. Hawkins, believe me that you'll find more of it than you can handle."

"There is no use you talking like this, Miss Willie," said Dabney Hawkins. "I'm sorry, but there isn't any man in this city going to tell this man he is drunk when I know I am not drunk. I would rather that man just tell me that he doesn't want to serve me than to lie about me. And that's all there is to it."

"Why didn't you just punch him in the damn nose, Mr. Hawkins?" asked Connie.

Augustina yelled at her again. "What do I have to do to convince you that I am very serious about that language of yours, Connie? Why is it necessary for you to use cuss words every time you open your mouth? Can't you just once sit at the table and be like your brother?"

"You just never hear him, Mom." Connie turned to Peter and said, "Tell Mom what you said to Mr. Tom in front of his store last week when he told you to go home!"

Peter turned to his mother. He wrinkled his dark brown eyebrows and said, "I wasn't anywhere near Mr. Tom's store. I was at the farm with Mamo."

"And when did you start going to the farm on Sunday afternoon?" asked Connie.

"I play with Snooks by the tin mill on Sundays, Sister."

"Talk about a lie!" Connie yelled to her mother. "Mr. Tom came running out of the store and told Peter and Snooks they were too small to play there, he was afraid one of his Sunday shoppers might trip over them and then he'd have one hell of a law suit on his hands. Snooks gave Mr. Tom the finger, and when Mr. Tom started to chase them away, Peter turned around, and I hope God strikes me dead right now if this isn't the truth, Mom, Peter told Mr. Tom he and his shoppers can go fuck themselves for all he cared!"

Willie Hawkins screamed, "Smack that girl! Smack that girl!"

With perfect timing Connie ducked her mother's spaghetti spoon. And when Augustina shouted, "Go to your room immediately!" no one at the table was surprised when Connie said, "I'm just repeating what Peter said to Mr. Tom!"

"Shame on you, girl!" Willie Hawkins yelled. "I hope you realize, Miss Augustina, she made that tale up. And her swearing to the Lord like that is likely to get us all struck down being near her!"

Augustina was still staring at Connie. "Did you hear me? I said to get upstairs! Come Saturday, I am going to leave you with Mrs. Major Hoffman and tell her to keep you at the headquarters until you learn to speak properly in front of people. And if it takes you the rest of the summer to stay there, that's fine with me. I can go to the tin mill myself with the baked goods. Now I do not want to hear another word from you this evening. I want you to get yourself upstairs this very second!"

Connie moved away from the kitchen table. She bumped into the corner of a cabinet, stumbled then righted herself and walked toward the stairwell. "The Mrs. Major! Ha! That dummy can't teach herself anything, let alone trying to teach me something."

Willie Hawkins threw her own spaghetti spoon at Connie. She hit Connie squarely on the back of the head leaving a wet patch of tomato sauce on the child's shiny black hair.

"I got her for you, Miss Augustina!" she boasted. "Lord! That child sure knows how to bring out the meanness in this woman!"

Wiping the sauce from the back of her head with the palm of her hand, Connie started to mount the stairs.

"I honestly believe," Willie Hawkins went on, "that child has no respect for anything or anyone."

"About as much respect as you have, Miss Willie," said Dabney Hawkins.

"Go ahead! Encourage that girl to continue with that mouth!" said Miss Willie.

"Well, darn it, Miss Willie!" exclaimed Dabney Hawkins. "I told you not to pay her any mind, didn't I?

You just upset the girl when you talk and she gets carried away. That child hardly touched her food, and now she won't be eating anything 'til tomorrow. Just keep quiet when you're around the girl."

"Oh! You're not much better than that child yourself. But I certainly will not have to worry about you much longer if you keep going into those downtown beer gardens."

"Are we back to that?" asked Dabney Hawkins.

They went on eating in silence until Willie Hawkins asked for another serving of spaghetti. "Peter," said Augustina, "please fill your grandmother's plate again. And you stay away from that river, young man," Augustina added. "You and Snooks are too young to play by that water."

"Yes, I know, Mom." Peter spooned more of the pasta onto Mrs. Vitello's dish. "Mr. Hawkins, why did the man at the saloon say you were drunk?"

"Because he didn't want to serve me, Sugar."

"Why?" asked Peter.

"Because I'm a colored man, Sugar. That's all." He laid down his fork and spoon while he spoke to Peter. "There are some white folks around the city who have the feeling that a colored man isn't fit to be in the same room with them." He started to smile. "But you're too young, Sugar, to go and start thinking about things like that. You'll understand what I'm talking about when you're a little older.

Peter moved his own plate over to the bowl and started to serve himself more spaghetti. "Am I colored, Mr. Hawkins?"

Dabney Hawkins smiled and said, "No, Sugar. You're not colored, son."

IV

On July 4th of every year, the FitzSimons family were hosts to the most elegant social event in New Castle. The polished gentry in evening dress, although the function began in the early afternoon, came from as far away as Chicago to attend Mr. and Mrs. FitzSimons' gala affair. A week before the event, the New Castle Daily Journal began bringing the tidings to the townspeople. For a week, the first page of the society section, which contained also the theatrical and the sports pages of the Daily Journal, broadcast the imminence of "prima-donna" entertainment from the New York stage and of a thirty-piece "well-balanced" symphonic orchestra from Canada, and passed on the rumor that an honored American general from the War of two years ago might be one of the guests of honor. The Daily Journal apologized for being unable to disclose the origins of its many accounts of the coming festivity, especially the "rumored" details. Still, it was common knowledge in the city that the FitzSimon's eldest son, Martin, was the general associate editor of the paper.

Willie Hawkins had worked at the social for the past two years; this year, at her recommendation, Augustina was added to the kitchen staff. Miss Willie lent her one of her white service dresses and a pair of white shoes; the shoes were a size too large, but the two women agreed upon toilet tissue stuffing as a solution to the problem.

"It just surprises me how I'm able to fit into your dress, Miss Willie," Augustina said on the morning of the Fourth.

Willie Hawkins studied the dress on Augustina. "We might've let out the shoulder seams a little," she said. "Is it uncomfortable, Miss Augustina?"

"It's just a wee bit tight under the arms, but it's only for the day."

Augustina turned to Connie. "This is a very important chance for us to make some extra money. And you know that we are going to need money to take Peter to Doctor Amos for his vaccination for school in September. So I don't need to tell you that I am counting on you to act and talk like a young lady."

"Don't worry about me, Mom," Connie assured her. "I promised you last night. I don't plan on embarrassing you or your friend."

"You better not complicate things for Miss Willie! It happens to be because of her and Mr. Hawkins that we have this chance at all, and that you have the chance to see the social."

"Please don't worry, Mom."

"You're the one who had better worry if you make any trouble," Willie Hawkins said.

And the only time Connie did cause a scene was when the Di Santangelos and the Hawkinses got onto the transit bus on the other side of the viaduct. Miss Willie and Mr. Dabney Hawkins got on first, followed by Peter and then Connie; finally Augustina helped her mother aboard. When Augustina tried to drop the coins for herself and Mrs. Vitello, the slot would not accept the nickels, and when Augustina spoke to the bus driver, he immediately turned and called out to Connie. "Hey, you, little girl! What did you put in this coin slot?"

Connie turned around, stared at him and said, "Are you talking to me?"

"Yes, I'm talking to you," the driver answered. "What did you put in here?"

"A nickel. What else?"

The driver looked back to Augustina. "The only time this machine jams is when someone puts a slug in it."

Augustina's face reddened. "Come up here, Connie. Now, have you started in already? What did you put in the coin box?"

Connie approached the front of the bus. "I told you. I put in a nickel. The one Mr. Hawkins gave me before we got on."

"Where did you put the nickel, little girl?" asked the driver.

Connie pointed to the side of the coin box. "In that slot, where else could you put it? And stop calling me 'little girl'!"

Augustina gave the driver the two nickels she had in her hand for herself and her mother, and then took a third coin from her purse and handed it to the driver. "I am so sorry," she said to him.

"Why are you doing that?" Connie snapped. "This guy's taking you for another nickel, Mom!"

"The reason is, Connie, because you were the last person to put whatever it was you put into this slot. And now the box is jammed and you heard what the driver said about the box jamming."

"But I put the nickel Mr. Hawkins gave me in the slot, Mom!"

"It really doesn't matter now, Connie. Please. Just go back in the bus with Mr. Hawkins. And don't let me catch you with a Hershey chocolate bar today."

When Connie joined the others at the rear of the bus, Willie Hawkins glared at her and asked, "What kind of trouble have you caused us already, girl?"

"I didn't cause any trouble. It's that bus driver who has problems from sitting on his goddamn brain day after day!"

At the FitzSimons' estate, Willie Hawkins led the group directly to the kitchen, where the head cook gave instructions to Augustina, Willie Hawkins and Connie, emphasizing that they should restrict themselves to the duties of the kitchen, and stay out of the way of the Chef-de-Cuisine. Dabney Hawkins was to work at his gardening as usual. Augustina instructed Peter to stay with Mrs. Vitello in the kitchen area and to make sure that neither of them got in the way of anyone, especially the Chef-de-Cuisine, who scowled at the group as if they were a bunch of vagabonds.

All morning Peter watched his mother and Willie Hawkins running around the huge kitchen, helping the cooks and the minor chefs. Occasionally, Connie's voice rose above the din of pots, pans and trays, shouting, "Move your ass, buddy, I'm coming through!" to one of the helpers, but she avoided the Chef-de-Cuisine, except to glance at him now and then and wink at Peter.

Eventually, the strains of the thirty-piece Canadian orchestra and the singing of the "prima donna" carried back to the kitchen. At the sound of the music, Mrs.

Vitello started tapping her foot, questioning Peter in rapid Italian about the food being served and the people dancing. Then, as the music rose higher, she fell silent, her sightless eyes blinking rapidly, her expression thoughtful; after a few minutes she began ticking items off on her fingers, one-two-three, as if counting her thoughts. Then, she asked Peter if he could see a clean pot or a large bowl that no one was using.

Peter looked around the huge kitchen and scanned a long counter. "Mamo," he said in Italian, "there is a large pot on the table and it has a big handle on it."

His grandmother gripped his arm firmly. "Is anyone looking at us?" she whispered.

Peter stared at her in wonder. "No," he said, "but many people are here in the kitchen."

Mrs. Vitello, squeezing his arm till it hurt, told Peter to wait until he was sure that no one was paying them attention, then to run and bring the pot back to her, and then to lead her to the ballroom.

"But Mamo," Peter whispered, "Mom will be very angry if we leave the kitchen!"

"You do as Mamo said, Peter."

Mrs. Vitello insisted that she knew what she was doing, and that Peter should just give the word when the time was right. And before Peter knew it, he and his grandmother were in the ballroom facing the FitzSimons' guests, Mrs. Vitello with her white cane and her left hand on Peter's shoulder, and Peter with the clean pot in his hand.

Mrs. Vitello told Peter to guide her to the orchestra, and they reached the podium just as the musicians finished a melody. She then told Peter to ask the conductor if it were possible for them to dance.

When Peter begged her to go with him back to the kitchen, she hit him with her cane, and then pushed him toward the conductor. When Peter explained to him what his grandmother wanted, he stared at them for a long moment. Then the conductor left the stand; Peter watched him as he went over to a very beautiful, elderly woman and spoke to her. The beautiful woman stood directly under a massive crystal chandelier which lit the entire ballroom. When she moved, the light from the chandelier caused her black silk dress to sparkle in a way which fascinated Peter who had never seen anyone as beautiful as Mrs. FitzSimons. The woman turned around and studied Mrs. Vitello and Peter, and then turned back to the conductor.

Returning toward the stand, the conductor walked up to Mrs. Vitello and said, "Mrs. FitzSimons has given her consent for you to entertain the guests if you so desire."

"Mamo doesn't speak English," Peter told him. In Italian, he said, "Mamo, it is all right to dance."

Speaking directly to Peter, the conductor asked, "Will you ask this Mamo what she wishes the orchestra to perform, young man?"

In Italian, Peter spoke to his grandmother, "Mamo, what should the band play?"

His grandmother replied in Italian, "Something lively, Peter. Please hurry!"

Peter translated to the conductor, who mounted the platform and huddled with the members of the orchestra.

At Mrs. Vitello's instruction, Peter set the white cane and the pot on the edge of the stage. Then the orchestra began the triumphal "Toreador Song" from Carmen. Peter guided his grandmother to the center of the ballroom floor, which had been cleared, chiefly because most of the guests were surprised by the musical selection.

As the orchestra played, Mrs. Vitello took Peter's hands into hers and began to spin him around and around in time to the music. She kept bending her body and sliding her feet rhythmically, and Peter was astonished by her quick, lively movements as she kept him spinning around her, neither one of them knew what in the world they were doing.

When the music slowed in the latter fourth of the selection, Mrs. Vitello pushed Peter down on the floor, and before he knew what was happening, she had his ankles in her hands and was heaving him forward to walk on his hands around the ballroom. She stepped on his right hand two or three times. Then, as they headed toward one of the ballroom walls, Peter cried out to her to turn around, but the music was too loud. She pushed him into the wall, banging his head. Mrs. Vitello sensed what had happened; she dropped one ankle, felt the wall with her hand, grabbed the ankle again, swung Peter and herself back toward the center of the floor, and danced on. Peter was holding his head with his left hand and started hopping across the floor on his right. As he watched the floor and the gawking guests leaning and tilting, he thought that perhaps his grandmother had gone mad. But when the music picked up its pace again, Mrs. Vitello dropped him and yelled at him to go get the pot and start collecting. His mouth dropped open, then he ran back to the orchestra platform and grabbed the pot, and while Mrs. Vitello kept whirling herself around the ballroom, Peter hurried up to the gentlemen guests and held out the pot.

They all threw in dollar bills and coins; one painfully thin lady frowned at her overstuffed husband, with the result that he dropped a few more dollars into the pot. Peter looked over his shoulder at his grandmother and saw her spinning toward another wall. He hurried across the floor, leaving the pot in its center, ran to Mrs. Vitello and quickly twirled her back toward the open surface. Then he ran for the pot and again started up the collection.

When the music stopped, the guests, as well as the members of the orchestra, gave them an amazing ovation, cheering and clapping. Peter waved and smiled while Mrs. Vitello shouted above the applause, "Grazie! Grazie!"

Mrs. FitzSimons came over to them and dropped a ten dollar bill into the pot. She smiled warmly at Peter, who thanked her.

"Oh, no darling," she said, still smiling. "My guests and I thank you and your dear friend for entertaining us." Peter was still intrigued by the beauty of the woman.

"She is my grandmother, and her name is Mamo."

Mrs. FitzSimons turned her smile to Mrs. Vitello. "Grazie, Mamo," she said to the old lady in black.

Mrs. Vitello bowed her head and replied, "Grazie, Signora. Grazie."

Peter retrieved his grandmother's cane, and as he directed her back toward the kitchen, he saw his mother, Willie Hawkins, and Connie, standing by the service entrance, their eyes as large as the half-dollar coins which lay among the bills in the pot. As Mrs. Vitello kept repeating "Grazie. Grazie", Peter led her past the others through the service entrance into the kitchen, and sat down with a great sigh.

On the way home from the FitzSimons' gala day, Augustina took Peter to task. "You and Mamo disappointed me very much today, Peter. You could have cost Miss Willie and Mr. Hawkins their jobs."

Then the twinkle in Willie Hawkins' eye ignited something in Augustina and both women began to laugh uncontrollably. "What in God's name could have possessed these two to behave like that? "Oh, dear!" Augustina laughed so hard that she could not say any more.

After they calmed down, Willie Hawkins suggested, "Why don't we go on a picnic soon, Miss Augustina, before summer is over and the kids go back to school?"

""Where, Miss Willie?" Peter leaned forward eagerly.

"I don't know, Sugar. What about Cascade Amusement Park, Miss Augustina?"

"It would be a nice day for the children," mused Augustina.

"Believe me, Miss Augustina, it would be a nice day for all of us," Willie Hawkins said, and then started to laugh again. "Did you see the way the Mamo was holding poor Sugar's ankles? And bouncing him off the wall like that!"

On Sunday Augustina and Willie Hawkins packed a large two-handled tomato basket with sandwiches, pizza slices, and oatmeal cookies, and the six of them went to the Cascade Amusement Park for the day. Peter sat between Dabney Hawkins and Connie on the tumblebug ride; Connie held her hands up off the safety bar and straight up in the air, screaming, "Feel that fucking wind, Mr. Hawkins!" Dabney Hawkins was not paying much attention to her. His mouth hung open with fright as the red and black tumblebug lurched and rumbled along the rail toward another dip in the ride.

Augustina and Willie Hawkins chased around the merry-go-round, trying to get Mrs. Vitello off the revolving platform, where she sat on a bench beating the daylights out of the nearest horse with her white cane. The slender boy on the horse held on for dear life, stared back at Mrs. Vitello and curled his legs up high toward the horse's neck, shrinking fearfully away from her cane.

V

Guiseppina Vitello died on Thursday, August 7th. Connie and her mother were in the kitchen, preparing the baked goods to take to the tin mill at the noon hour, when Peter came down the stairs and into the kitchen.

"Where's Mamo, Peter?" Augustina asked.

"Mamo won't get up," he said as he sat at the table.

Augustina stopped stirring the oatmeal cookie mix. "What do you mean, won't get up? Didn't you shake her?"

"I shook Mamo and I called her, but she won't get up," replied Peter. "Is the oatmeal ready?"

Augustina hurried toward the stairwell. Connie took over the stirring of the oatmeal-cookie mixture.

"The oatmeal's in the pan on the stove," she told Peter. "Get a bowl and I'll fill it up for you."

Augustina appeared at the head of the steps and yelled, "Connie! Go fetch Miss Willie and have her run over to Miss Libby and telephone Doctor Amos!"

Some time after Connie returned with Willie Hawkins, Dr. William Amos arrived and went upstairs to the large bedroom. Connie and Peter sat in the kitchen with Willie Hawkins and waited what seemed a very, very long time. Then they heard Augustina crying and calling, "Mom! Mom!" When Dr. Amos came down the stairs, he looked at Miss Willie Hawkins, shook his head, and walked out the kitchen door.

"Child," Willie Hawkins said to Connie. "You fix Sugar another bowl of oatmeal, and I'll go see Miss Augustina for just a minute. Don't either of you two move from this kitchen." She walked over to the kitchen door and snapped the lock. "I don't want Mr. Sam in this house at a time like this. Now don't either of you move from this room."

"Mamo kicked the old water bucket," Connie said to Peter.

"Hush that mouth, girl! And watch Sugar!"

Peter looked at Willie Hawkins for some sort of explanation. He knew, for one thing, that they never had a water bucket in their bedroom; it was always kept under the kitchen sink because his mother used it every Monday to fill the wringer-washer.

Peter was always bewitched on washday by the opposing rollers which squeezed water from the wet clothes, and when Augustina would notice his enraptured stare, she would entertain him by ducking the rinsed clothes back in the washer, then wringing them once again through the rollers. Water shot back into the washer, and Peter tilted his head to watch the clothes coming out the other side of the rollers.

Peter did not understand the idea of death, he was too young to grasp it. Augustina had tried to explain it to him when one of their neighbors had died the previous year. She told him that when people got very old, the Lord would call them home to Heaven because He loved them very much and wanted to take care of them because they were too old to take care of themselves. But Peter never understood Augustina's explanation, and now he just looked to Willie Hawkins for words. But Miss Willie walked over to the stairwell and mounted the steps.

Willie Hawkins stayed with the family all day, and in the late afternoon, when Dabney Hawkins came home from the FitzSimons estate, he joined them, and Miss Willie made supper for them all. Augustina had not yet come downstairs, and Connie and Peter had orders from Miss Willie not to go up; if they had to use the bathroom, they were to go over to the Hawkins' house.

As she served dinner, Miss Willie wiped her fore-head with her arm. "There is more food in the pan on the stove, Mr. Hawkins," she said in a tired voice. "Help the children when they're ready. I'm going up with Miss Augustina."

Dabney Hawkins looked up at his daughter. "You should eat something, Miss Willie. There isn't any sense in you getting sick over this. You won't be any good to Miss Augustina if you get sick."

"I'm not in the mood to eat just now, Mr. Hawkins," Miss Willie said, wiping her hands on an old cotton towel. "And I know Miss Augustina won't eat anything. I'll take a glass of water up to her. Just put the dishes in the sink, I'll wash them later. You take the children over to our place and bed them for the night, Mr. Hawkins."

Later, Dabney Hawkins did so. Miss Willie had de-cided to wait with Augustina for Mr. Di Santangelo's return from the clubs. Dabney Hawkins thought that it would be better for a man to talk to Mr. Di Santangelo about the death, but Willie Hawkins said that it would not make any difference. "Mr. Sam will be coming home half dead himself from drinking."

Dabney Hawkins took Peter and Connie into Willie Hawkins bedroom to bed them down for the night. As they sat up in Miss Willie's bed, Dabney Hawkins sat on an old rocking chair next to the dresser and near the window. He kept rocking forward and backward, occasionally pulling the lace curtain aside and looking out toward the Di Santangelo house.

Connie watched him rock and look out the window. "Why the hell are you peeking out the window every other second?"

"I'm looking out for Mr. Sam," Dabney Hawkins replied, letting go of the lace curtain. "There isn't any telling what he might do when he gets home. And there isn't anyone in that house except for Miss Augustina and Miss Willie. I'm just a little worried, child. I don't know. It's kind of hard to tell what a drunken man will do when he doesn't have his understanding together. Mr. Sam's a mighty mean creature, child, when he's been drinking. I hate to talk about Mr. Sam this way, him being your father, but you've seen Mr. Sam take after Sugar when he gets home, and you sure as heck have seen Miss Augustina in the morning after Mr. Sam has come home from a night of drinking."

"Will Mamo be coming home sometimes after she goes to Heaven, Mr. Hawkins?" asked Peter.

Connie looked at her brother, lying beside her in the bed, and then said, "Now I ask you, Mr. Hawkins, is Peter or is Peter about the dumbest kid in this neighborhood?"

Dabney Hawkins shook his head slowly and frowned at her. "What do you mean by 'is he or is he'? Now that's what I call a dummy, if you ask me. And that is no way to talk to your small brother. He's not to start his schooling until next month, and you're going into sixth grade. You should know better than to call Sugar names."

"My mother told me that God takes old people away to Heaven to take care of them, Mr. Hawkins," Peter said, "but she didn't say if they ever come back from Heaven. I never saw Miss India after she went to Heaven."

"And who told you that old witch went to Heaven?" asked Connie.

"Miss Willie did," replied Peter.

"That figures," Connie said.

"That is no way to speak about Miss India, girl." Dabney Hawkins went on, looking kindly at Peter, "When the Lord calls us, son, He doesn't give us back. It's not His way of doing things." He got up from the rocker and looked out the window once more, then started toward his own bedroom. "But, you can be sure, Sugar, that once the Lord calls you, He sure takes good care of you in Heaven."

When Dabney Hawkins returned to the children from his bedroom, he was carrying a small radio; he set it on the dresser and knelt down to plug it in.

"Are you praying for Mamo's soul?" Connie said in a smart aleck tone to Mr. Dabney. He ignored her, switched on the radio and slowly turned the selection dial. Connie went on, "Well, I sure as hell never want to die. It's too goddamn frightening to even think about it!"

Dabney Hawkins turned to face her. "You don't have any free will in that decision, child. When the Lord starts to calling you, you have to go. And if you want to go or if you don't want to, makes no difference to the Lord, because you're going." He found the local station carrying the Pittsburgh Pirates-Chicago Cubs game. "But there really isn't any sense talking to you about the doings of the Almighty, because you've made up your mind. And there isn't anything going to change it." He sat down and rocked slowly, looking out the window from time to time.

"I don't want to listen to any goddamn baseball game," said Connie. "My grandmother just died, and if you had any respect, you wouldn't be playing the radio."

"There isn't any sense in your using words like respect, child," said Dabney Hawkins. "If there is one word which the Lord left out of someone to understand, you're the one. And for all I care, you can go right to sleep and Sugar and me will listen to the game. There isn't anyone in this room forcing you to listen to the game."

Connie was not about to pay attention to the game. "Why didn't Miss Willie ever get married?" she asked.

"That's a question which you will have to ask Miss Willie," Dabney Hawkins replied.

But, actually, Willie Hawkins had married. One evening she told Augustina that she had kept company for almost two years with a gentleman caller from Suffolk that the minister had introduced to her at a church supper, and a week before Miss Willie was to get married, she ran away and got married to another gentleman friend whom she had never introduced as a caller to her family. But a year or so after she eloped, she returned with her suitcase to the Hawkins house, never explained anything to her father or mother, and began living with them again.

Finally, the first gentleman caller, Mr. Dennis Anthony, sort of swallowed his pride, so the Suffolk minister said, and began courting Willie Hawkins again. Everyone in the congregation approved, and in about six months, the church celebrated the marriage of Miss Willie Hawkins and Mr. Dennis Anthony. They headed for Cincinnati, where Mr. Dennis Anthony had gotten work in a brewery. But in a few months the couple returned to Suffolk, and according to Dabney Hawkins, Mr. Dennis Anthony came alone to the Hawkins home and informed Dabney Hawkins that he was returning Miss Willie to her parents because Willie Hawkins was just too much to handle.

"And although I know I made an oath to the Lord, and I don't have to tell you, Mr. Hawkins, that I would normally keep my end of the marriage bargain, but, sir, I believe I got the worst the good Lord ever made! A stubborn woman, sir. A mighty stubborn woman is Miss Willie! Now, I am going back to Cincinnati, Mr.

Hawkins, but I am sorry to tell you this, sir, but I am going back by myself. I give you back Miss Willie with the full blessing of the Almighty Lord!"

Willie Hawkins' mother was very disappointed in her daughter's conduct. By trying to argue and struggle against her daughter's nature, Mrs. Hawkins finally drove Miss Willie away from the house to live in the heart of the city of Suffolk in a rooming house for ladies only.

Every Sunday, Willie Hawkins would take a cab from the city to the Hawkins residence, near the peanut farm. But she always ordered the taxi driver to wait until she went into the house and saw how her parents received her. If the reception was anything but pleasant, Willie Hawkins would do a turnaround and backtrack out to the waiting taxicab. And she would not return until the following Sunday, when the cab driver would again wait outside for her judgement.

Eventually, Mrs. Hawkins took sick, and Willie Hawkins had to leave the boarding house and return home to take care of her mother and keep house for her father. And a few weeks later, she made just one pronouncement to her parents; that there was not one man on this earth who was good enough for Willie Hawkins. After that, no one mentioned the two marriages, or the possibility of the Lord seeing His way to provide a third gentleman caller for Willie Hawkins.

Seeing that Dabney Hawkins was going to say nothing further, Connie said, "If we listen to a baseball game, I want to hear Detroit and Cleveland. Detroit is going to take the World Series this year."

"You know that you're just saying that because Detroit won the Series in 1945," said Dabney Hawkins. "But the National League is going to take the Series this year. There is only one team, child, that took the pennant in 1942 and 1944, and that team will take the Series again, just like they did last year."

"The Cardinals!" yelled Connie. "No way will that bunch of lizards take it this year!"

"You just mark my words come this fall," said Dabney Hawkins.

"Then why don't we listen to the damn St. Louis game instead?" asked Connie. "I don't want to listen to the Pirates!"

"You know very well, child, we can only get the Pirate games on the radio here in New Castle."

"Well then all I can say to you, Mr. Hawkins, is piss on the Pirates and piss on your radio!" Connie turned her face toward the pillow and shut her eyes.

Dabney Hawkins and Peter sat listening to the game. At one point, Dabney Hawkins got up and went into his room, then returned with a large kitchen matchbox in his hand.

"Want to see my pet, Smitty, Sugar?"

Peter got out of bed and went over to the rocking chair. Dabney Hawkins eased the matchbox open and

Peter saw a grasshopper inside. Dabney Hawkins gently picked up the grasshopper and held it in his hand.

"Now look, Sugar," Dabney Hawkins said. "See how I have Smitty trained to sit on my hand. He won't jump off either. Here. Hold out your hand."

Peter looked quizzically from Dabney Hawkins to the green and brown insect and then cupped his hand and held it out. Dabney Hawkins cradled Peter's hand in his own and carefully placed the insect in Peter's small hand.

Peter peered intently at Smitty. He noticed a brown, wet spot on his palm.

"What's this brown spot, Mr. Hawkins?" he asked excitedly.

"Why that's tobacco juice, Sugar," Dabney Hawkins replied. "Smitty always leaves some on your hand when he's happy and especially if he likes you."

Suddenly, Peter's eyes widened. He raised his dark eyebrows and asked, "Does Smitty smoke, Mr. Hawkins?"

"No, son. Smitty eats the cigar and cigarette butts that people throw on the ground." He lifted the grasshopper from Peter's hand and put it back in the box, next to the radio, and sat down on the rocker. "Smitty sure likes them Lucky Strike cigarettes, Sugar. They're his favorite brand."

Peter settled himself comfortably on Dabney Hawkins' lap, occasionally picking up the box to look at Smitty, and listening to the baseball game.

The Pirates beat the Cubs three to nothing. The announcer said that the Cleveland-Detroit game had been called off because of rain in Detroit, and that St. Louis had walloped the Reds nine to two.

"St. Louis is too tough, Sugar. They're just too tough. Maybe next year, or the year after, you and me can take a train ride to Pittsburgh and go see the Pirates and St. Louis play."

Smitty continued spitting tobacco juice in the box. "Can we take Smitty with us on the train ride, Mr. Hawkins?" Peter asked just before he fell asleep on Dabney Hawkins' lap. Mr. Hawkins carried Peter back to the bed where Connie slept. He tucked the boy in next to his sister. He leaned over and gently kissed Peter on his cheek, and then went around Willie Hawkins' bed and kissed the sleeping Connie on her forehead. He stood for a moment looking down at the two children. Then shaking his head slightly he went back to the rocker. He looked out the window and saw that the light was now on in the kitchen of the Di Santangelo house. He jumped up, walked quickly out of the room, eased the door shut, and hurried down the stairs.

VI

As Dabney Hawkins entered the Di Santangelo's kitchen, he heard Mr. Di Santangelo's voice raging from upstairs. Fearfully, he hurried up the steps and into the large bedroom. What he saw there in the center of the room horrified him.

Mrs. Vitello was lying on the floor. Tenderly, Augustina held her dead mother's white head on her lap as, soundlessly, she wept.

"Mr. Hawkins!" Willie Hawkins shouted to her father. "Try and talk some sense into Mr. Sam! Get him the hell out of here and into the other bedroom!"

Mr. Di Santangelo glared drunkenly at Augustina

as she sat there helplessly holding her mother's head. "That whore always put her fucking mother before me!" he yelled to no one in particular. "Ever since the day we were first married. I never had a chance with those two whores around!"

Dabney Hawkins hurried toward him. "Mr. Sam! Good Lord, Mr. Sam! The Mrs. Mamo is dead. She died this morning. What are you doing to her?"

"I already told Mr. Sam that," shouted Willie Hawkins, shaking. "As soon as he came up the stairs! But he didn't hear me, Mr. Hawkins, he just shoved me over to the other side of the room! He didn't hear me! Please get him the hell out of here, Mr. Hawkins."

Dabney Hawkins walked over to Mr. Di Santangelo and put his hand on his arm. "There isn't any reason on earth for you to be in this room right now, Mr. Sam," he said. "Let us go into the other bedroom." He started to guide the scowling, swaying man, who nearly slammed into the doorway as he groped his way out of the room. "You have to get hold of yourself, Mr. Sam. Especially now. Miss Augustina has just lost the Mrs. Mamo. There isn't any use in you talking and hollering and calling names at a time like this."

He walked Mr. Di Santangelo toward the double bed in the adjoining bedroom. Mr. Di Santangelo knocked his shin against the seat of a wooden chair, then stumbled full into the chair and barely missed breaking the window it stood next to. He growled furiously, stood up, and kicked the chair in the opposite direction. "What you need right now is some good, sound sleep, Mr. Sam." Dabney Hawkins tried to guide Mr. Di Santangelo to sit on the bed. "You'll feel a heck of a lot better in the morning. Believe me, Mr. Sam, it isn't any good for you to go into the Mrs. Mamo's room and cause any more trouble. Leave Miss Augustina be, Mr. Sam. Please."

"They're both alike! Fucking whores! Both of them!"

"This talk isn't doing anyone any good. You have to try and get some sleep, Mr. Sam, and be ready for work tomorrow morning."

"Fuck sleep! Fuck work!" yelled Mr. Di Santangelo. "I hate this goddamn fucking dump and everything in it! I'm getting the fuck out of here right now!"

"No. You have to get some sleep, Mr. Sam," said Dabney Hawkins quietly as though he were speaking to a child. "There isn't anyone that's going to bother you in this bedroom. You've already had enough to drink, and you have to go to work first thing in the morning. Why don't you just lie across the bed and get some sleep, Mr. Sam?"

"Work for what? A whore who doesn't give a fuck about anyone but that dead piece of shit in the other room?" Mr. Di Santangelo turned and headed for the bedroom door. "No. I don't want to be in this house. I'm going down to Mahoningtown for the fucking night."

Though he was considerably smaller than Mr. Di Santangelo, Dabney Hawkins stood next to the swaying man, trying bravely to steady him so that he would not lose his balance. "If you want me to go with you, I'll walk with you down to Mahoningtown, Mr. Sam."

"To Mahoningtown?" Mr. Di Santangelo laughed sneeringly. A gargling cough interrupted his laugh. "How far do you think you'll get, being a nigger and walking through Mahoningtown?"

"There isn't anyone saying I can't walk to the end of the tin mill building, Mr. Sam," said Dabney Hawkins. "That is, if you don't mind walking with a colored man, Mr. Sam."

"No, Hawkins," said Mr. Di Santangelo. "It doesn't bother me to walk with any man."

Fearing that any second it might register upon Mr. Di Santangelo that the children were not in the house, Dabney Hawkins tried to hurry Peter's father as he helped him down the stairs and outside. As he walked beside Mr. Di Santangelo, Dabney Hawkins kept looking at his own house to be sure that no lights were on.

Together they walked out of the yard and down the main street that ran along the wall of the tin mill. Dabney Hawkins managed to keep a firm hold on Mr. Di Santangelo's arm as they walked together down the street. There was more than a little sadness in the voice of Dabney Hawkins as they walked along next to the tin mill that night. And the sadness that reached down into him was reflected also in his face for Dabney Hawkins knew that Mr. Sam heard little of what was being said to him.

"I think you know me pretty well, Mr. Sam. I'm not the one to be questioning or troubling other people about what they do, and I don't feel I have a right to pass judgement. That is up to the Lord on Judgement Day. But I am worried about what might happen if you keep drinking like you do, Mr. Sam. Mind you, now, I'm not passing judgement on your drinking. There's a difference, Mr. Sam. But, I am concerned about Miss Augustina and the children. They have a hard time making ends meet, and now with the Mrs. Mamo gone like this, I don't really know what Miss Augustina is going to do."

"She can do any fucking thing she wants to do, Hawkins. If she wants to fuck the whole neighborhood for money, that's fine with me. I just don't want to have anything to do with that piece of shit!"

"Well, it's not for me to go and agree with what other people say," Dabney Hawkins said. "And if that's the way Mr. Sam feels, I guess that's the way Mr. Sam feels. But to tell you the truth, I think Miss Augustina is one fine woman. She works hard putting food on the table for the family."

When, finally, they reached the end of the tin mill, Mr. Hawkins stopped short. "I can't go with you any farther than this block, Mr. Sam. You know the ruling of the people of Mahoningtown. But, you know that you're more than welcome to go with me over to Mr. Adams' Tavern for a drink. We can talk a little, and sort of think things out about you and the family. I hear tell, Mr. Sam, that sometimes if a person has somebody to talk to, a thing or two might come out to do some good."

"No, Hawkins. I'm going down to one of the clubs in Mahoningtown."

"You do believe me, don't you, Mr. Sam, that you are more than welcome to drink at Mr. Adam's? The Lord knows there isn't any uninvited rule in this neighborhood. I would like to talk to you, for a while, Mr. Sam. It just doesn't seem right to be next door neighbors and we never have sat down to have a good talk. I could use a beer myself, now that I think about it. Hell, we can stay there all night and drink up a storm if that's what you want to do."

"You better go back, Hawkins, 'cause I'm heading for Mahoningtown," said Mr. Di Santangelo. And though he looked directly at Dabney Hawkins with his menacing, dark eyes as he spoke; at the same time, it did not seem that Mr. Di Santangelo ever really saw the small, kindly black man to whom he spoke. As Samuel Di Santangelo walked unsteadily away from his neighbor, Dabney Hawkins, he muttered grudgingly not so much to himself as to the anonymous night air which surrounded the tin mill. "I just want to be by myself. I just want to be by myself."

Then finally, in silence, Mr. Di Santangelo stepped slowly down Cedar Street toward Mahoningtown, his head drooping as he walked.

Dabney Hawkins called helplessly after him, "You sure you won't change your mind, Mr. Sam?" But his words fell emptily on the night air of New Castle, Pennsylvania. Mr. Di Santangelo kept walking. He did not look back. "Mr. Sam?" called Dabney Hawkins. The small man stood quite still at the corner of Cedar and Mahoning Avenue, the end of the tin mill site, and watched the figure of Mr. Di Santangelo until it gradually disappeared from sight. Then, resignedly, he turned and retraced his steps hurriedly back to the Di Santangelo house.

He rushed up the stairs. As he entered the bedroom, he called to his daughter, "You get the Mrs. Mamo's feet, Miss Willie, and I'll get her shoulders, and we'll lift her onto the bed."

Augustina still sat crying pathetically and holding her mother's head in her aproned lap. Dabney Hawkins went to her and laid his hand lovingly on her head and said almost in a whisper to her, "Miss Augustina, why don't you go over to the bed and sit a few seconds while Miss Willie and me get the Mrs. Mamo back on the bed?"

Augustina did not move. Dabney Hawkins and Miss Willie helped her off the floor and guided her to sit on

Connie's bed. Then, they lifted the dead Mrs. Vitello onto the double bed which the old woman had so recently shared with her beloved grandson, Peter.

Willie Hawkins fetched a wet wash cloth from the bathroom and began to wipe Mrs. Vitello's face. Miss Willie was still visibly shaken from what she had just witnessed. "Mr. Sam just came in here and started to yell at Miss Augustina and the Mrs. Mamo. I told Mr. Sam that the Mrs. Mamo had died, but Mr. Sam wouldn't listen to a word. Mr. Sam just kept yelling and cussing at Miss Augustina until he made the air blue in this bedroom! And then Mr. Sam went over to the bed, grabbed the Mrs. Mamo, picked her up and threw the Mrs. Mamo right on the floor! Right in front of Miss Augustina, he threw the Mrs. Mamo right on to the floor. I would never have believed it, had I not seen it with these own eyes, Mr. Hawkins!" Having said this, Willie Hawkins shook her head and her eyes registered absolute disbelief in what she had seen.

When Willie Hawkins finished wiping Mrs. Vitello's face, she went to Augustina, put her arms around her and guided Augustina's head to her shoulder. "Why don't you get some sleep, Miss Augustina? Mr. Sam won't be back tonight. And Miss Willie will stay here with you and the Mrs. Mamo."

"I'll stay here, Miss Willie," Dabney Hawkins said softly. "You better get some rest yourself. You can go on over to the house and use my bedroom."

"No, I'm not leaving this woman, Mr. Hawkins. You best just go over and stay with the children. And lock the doors to both houses."

"I don't think Mr. Sam will be coming back tonight," Dabney Hawkins said.

"Just don't take any chances. Lock the doors to both the houses. How are the children?"

"They're both sound asleep in your bed," Dabney Hawkins said. "I'll go over now and check on them. If you need anything, you just raise that window and yell out to me," he said pointing to one of the bedroom windows. "I'll be right there on your rocker and I'll have the window up a little bit, so I'll hear you if you call."

He headed for the bedroom door, then turned around and looked with compassion at the two women, his daughter, Willie, and her dear friend, Augustina.

"Go ahead, Mr. Hawkins," Willie Hawkins said. "Don't worry about Miss Augustina and Miss Willie. We'll be all right. Go on, now."

Dabney Hawkins left the bedroom and went down the stairs. He snapped the lock, carefully, as he closed the kitchen door.

He entered his own house and locked it just as carefully as he had locked the house he just left, then he climbed the stairs to Willie Hawkins' bedroom to see to Connie and Peter. He walked over to the dresser and peered out the window which he then raised a few inches. He sat down, tiredly, in the rocking chair and listened to the soft, sleeping sounds of the children in Willie Hawkins' bed. He stayed at the window and kept a vigilant eye on the kitchen porch of the Di Santangelo house.

VII

Willie Hawkins sat next to Augustina on Connie's bed. She spoke gently but firmly to her friend. "You know, Miss Augustina, that you cannot go on living like this," she said. "You have to give some serious thinking about Mr. Sam and his behavior toward you and Sugar. After what I saw this evening, Miss Augustina, I'm frightened."

"My poor mother, is she all right over there, Miss Willie?" Augustina asked.

"Yes, I washed her face with a wash cloth. The children are bedding with Mr. Hawkins over at our place, and I'll be here with you. Close your eyes and try to find sleep."

"God, I have never in my life seen Sam act like this," Augustina said. "Sam was never like this 'til he started drinking. Who would have ever believed this could happen to Sam?" She lifted her head abruptly from Willie Hawkins' shoulder. "Do you still have the wash cloth, Miss Willie?"

"I have to rinse it." She returned in a moment with the wet wash cloth in her hand. "You just lie back and I'll wipe your face, Miss Augustina."

"That's all right. I'm able to do it."

"I'm not saying you're not. But it isn't necessary for you to do it when I'm here, now is it?" Miss Willie ran the cool cloth over Augustina's forehead and around her eyes. "Why don't you try to get some sleep now, Miss Augustina?"

"Oh, I can't sleep." Augustina turned her head toward the other bed and looked with great sadness at her mother. "Poor, poor Mamo," she said.

"Everything is going to be all right. Just rest a spell, please."

"She had such a hard life, Miss Willie," Augustina said. "My sister Annie died at eighteen in childbirth. The baby died too. I was only fourteen then and five years later they found my father on the floor of the tin mill. He died of a heart attack. Within six months my sister, Jenny, died from diphtheria. I questioned the Lord then, Miss Willie. You know, Miss Willie, some people have to carry wooden crosses through life while other people have to carry concrete crosses. I was bitter. How did my mother keep her sanity? She wanted to go back to Italy, but the funerals just took everything we had. The tin mill gave us just enough money to bury my father, and after we buried Jenny, we had nothing left. God is so unfair at times!"

Willie Hawkins listened to Augustina as she continued to wipe her face and neck. "You must not question the ways of the Master, Miss Augustina. Now is the time to put your faith in God to help you and your children through this tragedy. During times of misfortune, we must never question the Almighty, Miss Augustina."

"Oh, but I have to question Him, Miss Willie. It was so cruel, my mother losing her daughters and her husband in so short a time. She was such a good person, Miss Willie, and never, never did she deserve such punishment."

"The Lord does things in a dark, unknown, mysterious way sometimes, but we must never lose faith in Him. Without God, we are nothing, Miss Augustina. You must never lose faith."

"But what did my mother ever do to God?"

"The Mamo was a good woman. She is at peace now. She has seen God, she has spoken to Jesus. And she is walking in the Garden of Heaven with her husband, her daughters and her parents. You must not feel sorry for the Mrs. Mamo, Miss Augustina. She has gone home to be with the people she has not seen for a very, long time. If you feel hurt, Miss Augustina it is only because you know that you will not see the Mrs. Mamo again on this earth. But you will see her again when you get to Heaven. And you must be very happy for the Mrs. Mamo, for she is with the Lord in His Kingdom."

"I don't know what to feel anymore, Miss Willie."

"You're tired and you should try to rest. I don't want to hear you talking like this, Miss Augustina. God and the Lord are all I live for, and you hurt Miss Willie when you question my Master. I just live for the day that I can see God face to face, and talk to my Jesus, and dwell in the happiness of Paradise."

Because of her exhaustion and confusion, Augustina seemed to remove herself as she began to reminisce and to speak of her husband Sam, of how greatly she had loved him, of how drastically he had changed.

"Sam was so handsome when I first knew him, Miss Willie. I remember when my best friend, Florence, took me to a softball game and introduced him to me. I had not dated much and so I had a hard time speaking to him. But, eventually, he began to come over to the house and we started to date.

He was so patient with me. I was plain then , I didn't even how what makeup was let alone how to wear it. I was bashful. Sam was so sensitive to what had hap-pened to our family. One day he just proposed to me out of the blue. My mother was so happy for me. Oh, to think how much my mother loved Sam and then to see him throw her on the floor this evening."

"Please, Miss Augustina. There isn't any sense in looking back now."

Augustina continued in spite of her friend's pleadings. "In 1941, after Peter was born, Sam tried to enlist in the Army but was rejected because of a heart murmur. All of his friends enlisted but poor Sam was rejected, Miss Willie. It nearly killed him."

Tears flowed unrestrainedly down Augustina's checks as she spoke now. Willie Hawkins wiped her checks with the wash cloth and tried to calm her.

"Please, Miss Augustina. Don't do this to yourself."

"I was happy that he was rejected, Miss Willie. I didn't want him to go and leave us but it was all part of menfolk's vanity that they had to help their country in time of war. It was then he took to drinking. The tin mill was hiring women all around him. He listened to them talk of their husbands and boyfriends going off to war and it was too much for him, Miss Willie. Sam would come home at night and go straight to our bedroom without eating. I would try to talk to him but he would just look at me with tears in his eyes and say nothing. I would go into the kids' room and cry for Sam. I loved him so much, Miss Willie. I still do love him."

"I don't question your feelings toward Mr. Sam, Miss

Augustina," Willie Hawkins said, "but I am frightened by his behavior toward you and Sugar."

"It's not Sam, Miss Willie, it's the drinking. He went back for another physical and when he was rejected a second time, it was too much for him. That was when Sam really took to drinking. He quit coming home some nights, and when he did come home, he was so drunk that he took to swearing out loud and of all things, Miss Willie, claiming that Peter was not his child! How could he have thought such a thing, Miss Willie? I have never known another man except Sam."

"I don't think you have to tell Miss Willie anything like that, Miss Augustina."

"Finally, Sam's behavior was so bad and the swearing too that we became the outcasts of the Italian neighborhood. We were evicted because of what was happening. And, since Sam was drinking all our money away, Mom and I took the cheapest place we could find for the sake of the children's having a home, at least. And then three years ago, my mother went blind because of diabetes. Sam just became uncontrollable. Things just kept piling up and up. It's a wonder we haven't been thrown out of this neighborhood too."

"That's nonsense talk, Miss Augustina."

Augustina seemed suddenly to take hold of herself. She calmed down and asked Willie Hawkins, "Will you stay here with my mother tomorrow while I go to St. Jude's to make funeral arrangements?"

"Miss Willie will be right here when you return from the church tomorrow, Miss Augustina, just don't you worry." Augustina touched Willie Hawkin's arm. "I don't know what my mother and I would have done if we didn't have you and Mr. Hawkins as our next door neighbors, Miss Willie."

"It works both ways. The Lord sees to that, Miss Augustina. There isn't a day that goes by that you aren't over at our house dropping something off that you didn't sell at the tin mill. Your family has a lot of love in it, Miss Augustina, a lot of love."

She continued to wipe Augustina's face and neck. "I was thinking when you were telling me about the people in Mahoningtown running you out like that. Lord, I can just picture those people in church every Sunday. But, we have a few of the same type in our church too, Miss Augustina. Sometimes I sit in the church before the service and watch them, and I say to myself, 'How do these people do it? Acting so evil in so many shortcomings, and then putting on airs here in the church, and then leaving the church to go back to their evil ways.' And then I ask my Lord to forgive me for my thoughts, because I know that I have no right to pass judgement on my sisters and my brothers. And, I guess if people have to be that way, the best place for them is in the church. At least they are not causing any pain for about an hour or two for somebody."

"I agree with you, Miss Willie."

"Why don't I go downstairs and make a pot of coffee or a cup of tea now?"

"Coffee sounds fine, Miss Willie."

"Do you think you can eat some toast?"

"No, the coffee is fine."

"It won't take long. Now you just lie there and rest."

As Willie Hawkins was leaving the room, Augustina smiled slightly and called out to her, "Miss Willie?"

"Yes?"

"God bless you, Miss Willie."

"God bless you, Miss Augustina."

VIII

On Friday morning, Augustina went over to the Hawkins house and instructed Connie to go and stay with Willie Hawkins at the Di Santangelo house, but not to go into the bedrooms. She thanked Dabney Hawkins for the care of her two children, and took Peter with her to St. Jude's Roman Catholic Church located in the south side area of the city of New Castle to see the pastor about Mrs. Vitello's funeral. They waited in the rectory for some time until Father Donovan had time to see Augustina.

Augustina and Peter sat on two large chairs in front of the rectory desk. Behind the desk sat Father

Donovan, a heavy-set priest whose neck bulged over his white Roman collar. He wore glasses which were a little tight for his plump face, and his hands were folded together on the large, highly-polished desk.

"There is absolutely nothing that St. Jude can do for you, Augustina," Father Donovan said smugly, leaning over the desk, after listening to Augustina's account of her mother's death and her request for the Catholic legitimization of the funeral service. "You don't have the finances to pay for a low mass. It's as simple as that."

"But, Father," pleaded Augustina, "I do have some money, and I'll be able to get the rest for you in about three months."

"I am truly sorry, but I am unable to help you. We are not running some type of an organization, Augustina, which specializes in raising and expending parishioners' offerings for some sort of public burial for people as your mother. And what in the Lord's name, may I ask, possessed you to come here instead of going to one of the two churches in Mahoningtown?"

"I couldn't go there, Father, because of the people and their reaction to my family's situation. They had us evicted from Mahoningtown, and my family has been attending mass here at St. Jude's for the past three years."

Father Donovan pulled a cigarette out of an engraved box on the desk, and lit it with a gleaming lighter. "Well, I certainly am aware of the people you are associated with since you left the Mahoningtown parish, Augustina. What type of reaction are our people going to have when they see all of those colored people coming into our beloved church? You cannot expect St. Jude's to allow such a spectacle! Surely you realize this, don't you, Augustina? You are going to have to be reasonable. We have been trying to get our parishioners to contribute more to the new school fund, and you certainly don't want to jeopardize such a plan for our children, do you?" He looked sternly at Peter. "Does your son go to school, Augustina?"

"Peter will start the first grade next month, Father."

"I assume at the Mahoningtown public school?"

"No, father. He will be going to Lincoln-Garfield."

"Will this son of yours attend St. Jude's when we start our school in 1950?" Father Donovan asked.

"I don't know, Father, I would love to see Peter attend St. Jude's, but I don't know if I will have the funds to send him to school."

Father Donovan shook his head and smiled condescendingly. "Yes, of course. The funds. And here you are demanding a thirty-five dollar mass for your mother. Oh, dear, dear, Augustina. Please be reasonable."

"I don't think I am demanding, Father. I assure you that I will be able to pay for the mass. I can get the money for you, but it will take a little time."

"May I inquire as to the type of casket, if any, you are planning to bring into the church, Augustina?"

Father Donovan asked, looking at her contemptuously.

"I'm sorry, Father," Augustina said. "But everything has been happening so fast, that I haven't given much thought about..."

"Of course you haven't," Father Donovan interrupted. "And do you want to know why? Because you do not have the money for a casket. You see, Augustina, you have come to me unprepared for what you are seeking. Where are you going to bury your mother? In St. Jude's cemetery? Do you have any concept at all what the price of a burial plot is, Augustina? Where are you going to get the money to purchase the headstone marker? Where in God's name are you going to find money for the things you want to do for your mother, Augustina?"

Father Donovan smiled continually as he spoke to Augustina and his tone of voice was that of an adult who is tolerating the behavior of a difficult child. There was no trace of compassion in his speaking or in his behavior. He looked directly at Augustina never averting his eyes from her. But, more than once, Augustina averted her eyes from the eyes of Father Donovan. The color in her cheeks was high as she tried to cover her embarrassment. Peter sat by his mother's side throughout the conversation looking from the priest to his mother as they spoke. But, he did not understand.

"Please, Father. All I am asking for is that you provide a low mass for my mother. Please, Father. My mother was a very religious Catholic, Father."

"I am not judging the fact that your mother was a good Roman Catholic or a bad Catholic, Augustina, but did your mother or even you, ever contribute anything to St. Jude's in the years that you have walked into our church for mass?"

"We couldn't afford to give money to the church—"

"No." Father Donovan interrupted, leaning forward dramatically in his chair and coming closer to Augustina's face. "You could not afford to give to the church. And you cannot afford it now. You do realize that you are talking about six to nine hundred dollars for a mass, casket, burial plot and marker, do you not?"

Father Donovan opened the box, pulled out another cigarette and lit it. He looked at Augustina, and said, "Believe me, Augustina, I am not asking these things to hurt you. I am only trying to be quite honest with you. You and your mother did not support our church and if all of our parishioners were as irresponsible as your family has been toward our church, there would be no St. Jude's"

Father Donovan put his right hand to his forehead for a few seconds, and studied Augustina. He then spoke in an authoritarian manner. "I cannot help you as far as a low mass here at St. Jude's. If you are still entertaining the notion of a service for your mother, I am willing to attend the grave site for a small prayer service. But certainly not at St. Jude's cemetery. You will have to bury your mother in some other cemetery in the city. You can telephone the city office and they may be able to assist you. And, I will only charge you fifteen dollars for the entire prayer service."

Having thus made his final pronouncement, Father Donovan placed his hands palms down, rings up, upon his desk. He removed his plump bottom pompously from the chair in which he had been wedged. He peered, unwaveringly, over the tops of his glasses, which had somehow escaped their confinement and managed to slip down to the bridge of his shiny nose, at the gentle woman who had come to him and asked with the greatest humility for his help in the burial of her beloved mother.

Augustina listened quietly to Father Donovan's proclamation. She arose from her chair, took Peter's small hand in her own and said, respectfully, to the priest, "Thank you, Father. I will contact you this afternoon, as soon as I make arrangements at a cemetery." Augustina was tired, defeated and depressed. Somehow, Peter seemed to sense his mother was upset, though he was too young to understand what had cause it.

Peter walked closely by Augustina's side as they left the rectory.

And as they left, Peter noticed a large crucifix with a replica of the figure of Christ gazing toward Heaven, in front of the rectory. It reminded Peter of the crucifix that his grandmother had worn on her white apron, and of the wooden cross his grandmother had on the wall over their large double bed at home. Peter kept staring at the rectory's large crucifix as he and his mother departed St. Jude's Roman Catholic Church. As always, he was especially aware of the raw, bleeding wounds on the hands, feet and chest of Jesus. It would be years from this day before Peter would understand the true meaning of this figure of Christ, and the words He spoke to His Father, as He gazed toward Heaven from the Cross.

Augustina and her son headed for Moravia Street and the viaduct, which led them to the black neighborhood of the city, and to their home.

IX

Mrs. Vitello was buried the following day. Willie Hawkins and Dabney Hawkins made arrangements with their minister at the First Baptist Christ Church, not only for a plot in its cemetery, but also for permission to display Mrs. Vitello's pine casket in the church for a couple of hours so that the people of the neighborhood could pay their final respects to the "old white woman" who lived in their section of the city.

Mr. Tom took up a collection at the general store, while his wife, Miss Libby, went around the black neighborhood collecting enough funds for the casket. And Mrs. Major Hoffman, whom Willie Hawkins had telephoned from Mr. Tom's store after Augustina had stopped at the Di Santangelo house with a report on the meeting with Father Donovan, assured Willie Hawkins that she would provide the fifteen dollars out of her own pocket for the priest's services. But Mrs. Major Hoffman suggested that Dabney Hawkins, rather than she, herself, give the money to Father Donovan at the grave site.

All morning long, the people from the black neighborhood went into the First Baptist Christ Church to see Augustina and bid farewell to Mrs. Vitello. Mrs. Major Hoffman attended the funeral visitation at the church and sat with Augustina and her children until it was time to depart for the cemetery, and only after she gave Mr. Dabney Hawkins the fifteen dollars for Father Donovan did she leave the Di Santangelo family and head for the viaduct.

Willie Hawkins stood by Augustina, and Dabney Hawkins held the hands of Connie and Peter. They followed the six black pallbearers out of the church and walked to the cemetery, to await the arrival of Father Donovan, who appeared a half hour late. When he did arrive, the priest strolled ceremoniously to the casket and conducted the solemn Catholic prayer ritual for the deceased from the Catholic church manual.

After completing the service, he turned and spoke to Augustina in his most smoothing priestly voice. "I do not have to tell you, Augustina, that your dear mother is now on the right hand of the Lord. For she was a good Christian woman and a good person on God's earth. And, although she will be missed by you and your family, and the people at St. Jude's Church, you must always remember that Mrs. Vitello had lived a long life on earth, and since she is now in the hands of the Lord, it is best for you to devote your sadness to praying for her eternal soul." He waited and looked at Augustina, who was kneeling by the casket with Willie Hawkins standing by her side. When the priest cleared his throat, Dabney Hawkins went up to him and gave him the fifteen dollars.

"I don't know what the Lord wants His children to do for Him, sir," Dabney Hawkins whispered to Father Donovan. "But I do know that we must all stand in front of the Master on Judgement Day. If there is one thing He must want from His children, I would think that it would be for us to help the less fortunate of His children. Yes, sir, I strongly believe that is what the Master would want from his children."

Dabney Hawkins looked long and hard at Father's Donovan's long, black automobile, and then turned back to the priest. "You don't need that fifteen dollars I just gave you, sir," he said unemotionally. "Please give it to Miss Augustina for food for the two children?"

Father Donovan, unmoved, looked disdainfully at Dabney Hawkins. He put the fifteen dollars in his pocket, turned on his heel and left the cemetery for his automobile.

The people waited at the grave site until Willie Hawkins thought it was time for everyone to leave. She then took Augustina by the shoulders and stood her on her feet.

Augustina started to cry. "Please, Miss Willie. I want to stay just a while longer."

"It is time for us to go, Miss Augustina," Willie Hawkins said firmly. "There isn't any reason for us to stay here at the cemetery. These men have some work to do here. Let us go home, now."

Augustina continued crying. "No! Please, Miss Willie! Please let me stay with my mother for a little longer!"

Willie Hawkins turned to the people who were gathered around the grave site. She nodded her head, a signal for them to start an extremely slow clapping of the hands and a faint humming. The pallbearers stood near the casket, waiting for Augustina and her family to depart.

Augustina screamed a bone-chilling, "No! Oh, God, no!" She tried to break Willie Hawkin's grip, but Willie Hawkins clung to her and pulled her little by little away from the burial site, urging her quietly to come with her as she did so. Augustina, aware only of her deep-felt sorrow, continued to wail. "Stop it, Miss Willie! Let me be! Don't make me leave my mother! Please! Oh, God, please!"

"Come. There is nothing for us to do except to go home, Miss Augustina," Willie Hawkins said, as the slow, rhythmic clapping and the soft humming of the people continued. "Let us go, Miss Augustina. These gentlemen have a job to do."

"No! I won't leave my mother!" shouted Augustina, fighting to break Willie Hawkins' hold.

"Miss Libby!" yelled Willie Hawkins to Mr. Tom's wife.

Miss Libby ran up to Willie Hawkins and put her arms around Augustina.

"Now we are going, Miss Augustina," Willie Hawkins said again. "And we're going right this minute."

Willie Hawkins and Miss Libby took Augustina by the arms and escorted her out of the cemetery. Dabney Hawkins followed the three women. On his left side walked Peter, holding tightly to his older friend's hand; while on his other side a subdued Connie walked quietly along. She too clung tightly to the hand of this slight, black man whose marked gentleness at such a time spoke more vividly than words of his mortal strength.

X

School was to start within a month, and Augustina, with the help of Willie Hawkins and Mrs. Major Hoffman, began to prepare Peter to enter the first grade. Augustina intended to seek a full-time job when Peter was in school, and when she went for interviews during the beginning and mid-parts of August, she always wore her blue and white polka dot dress. Peter stayed then quite happily with Willie Hawkins.

As Peter made himself ready for his first year of schooling during August of 1947, Connie decided to turn over a 'new leaf'. Her decision was not an easy one but one which, though she didn't know it, she made for love of her brother. "Peter," she said to him one day, "I have decided that from now on I will not ever call you 'shit head' again."

Peter's eyes widened at this unexpected good news. He hunched forward a little from his position on the bank of the Shenango River where he was sitting with his legs crossed 'Indian style'. He propped his elbows on his knees, cupped his chin in his hands and a tiny smile played on his face. "Thank you, Sister." he said in a muffled tone hardly moving his lips as he spoke.

"Peter, when you start school next month," continued Connie somewhat imperiously as she paced back and forth, "you must not be ashamed of what you wear. I know that I bitched a lot about the dresses Mamo made for me, but that doesn't count because most of the time I was just joking." She tossed a stone into the river and continued. "Listen, Peter, they have some shitty things over at the school that will hurt you for a while, but believe me, you'll have to just not worry about them, and like the Mrs. Major always said to us, to adjust, like me and Jimmy Bobjack and the other colored kids at school had to do."

Suddenly, she stopped pacing. She leaned down and gazed directly into her brother's eyes so that he would have to understand exactly what she was saying. She continued. "I'll only be at the school for your first year, and then me and Jimmy Bobjack will be going to Ben Franklin. You and Snooks will be on your own when you get to the second grade, and you two will have to stick together and help each other out."

Peter would glance now and then at the Shenango River. Connie was not sure that he was hearing her so that every so often she would take hold of his chin and turn his face toward her, and she would talk right into his face. "Did you hear me, Peter? You and Snooks will really have to stick together! It'll be a lot harder on Snooks than it will be for you, Peter, because he's a colored boy. And you're going to have to keep an eye out for Snooks and help him if he gets into any trouble. I have to do the same thing with Jimmy Bobjack Hunter down at Lincoln."

Suddenly, Peter wrinkled his brows. "Why does Jimmy Bobjack have so many names, Sister?" Peter asked very seriously as he continued sitting 'Indian style' on the river bank.

"Oh, Peter, please," Connie responded in desperation at the trivial nature of his question. "We're talking about important things here!"

She stood, looked toward the house, and then sat back down on the river bank, pulled a cigarette from her pocket, and lit the cigarette.

"Sister! If Miss Willie sees you smoking, she'll tell Mom," Peter said excitedly.

"Fuck Miss Willie!"

"Why do you use that word all the time, and why does Mom get mad when you say it?" asked Peter. "Mom told Miss Willie to hit you if Miss Willie ever heard you use that word. What does it mean?"

"It doesn't mean anything, Peter," Connie replied. "Just don't tell Mom, what I said, or that you saw me smoking."

"I won't say anything, Sister," Peter answered. He picked up a stone, and tossed it into the river, imitating Connie. "Is Mom a whore, Sister?"

"What!" Connie exclaimed. She looked at her brother. "No, Peter, Mom's not a whore."

"What does whore mean?" Peter asked.

"It doesn't mean anything," Connie replied.

"Dad always calls Mom a whore, Sister. And he called Mamo a whore, too."

"That's only because Dad drinks too much, and he doesn't know what he's saying when he's drunk."

"Well, what does it mean?"

"I already told you, Peter, it doesn't mean anything," Connie said. "It's just a bad word like the word fuck. And just because Dad uses that stupid word doesn't mean you have to use it. You shouldn't use that word, Peter, because it is a very bad word, even though it doesn't mean anything. I promise to never use the word fuck again if you promise to never use that word again, especially in front of Mom."

"The word whore?"

"Yes. Promise?"

"I never said it in front of Mom, Sister."

"I know you haven't, Peter, but I want to make sure that you never say it in front of Mom, or anyone else."

"I promise not to say it again, Sister," Peter said. "And, I'm glad Mom's not a whore. Mamo wasn't a whore, was she?"

"Peter!" yelled Connie. "You promised not to use that word! And, no, Mamo wasn't one either. Now, listen to what I am saying to you about the school. Every day most of the white kids in the school take a milk break, and the kids that don't have the money to buy the little bottles of milk are instructed by the teacher to put their head on top of their arms and rest on their desk, and take a morning nap during the milk break period, and Mom can't afford to give you the money for the milk, Peter. The only good thing about it, Peter, is that the bottles are so damn small, I wouldn't pay a dumb dime for one, even if I had a dime.

"Another thing is the Wednesday morning savings plan at the school, Peter. The teacher lines up the white kids in front of her desk, and collects a quarter, or fifty cents, from each kid and the school puts the money into a savings account at the bank. Now the best thing to do, Peter, when this happens at the school, is to practice your reading and pay the other kids no mind, especially the types like Patty Ann Johnson, who carries her savings book around with her all day so the other kids can see she isn't one of the poor kids at Lincoln. She even takes it with her during recess!"

Connie tossed the cigarette into the river. "And, besides that, Peter, the colored kids, and some of the poor white kids, always get the beat-up textbooks, because the teachers always give the newer books to the properly dressed white kids. But the used books are the best ones anyway, because you don't have to worry about taking care of them since they're all.." she squinted at Peter, "..screwed-up to begin with. Do you understand what I'm saying, Peter?"

"Yes, Sister," Peter answered. "I'll give my good book to Snooks."

"No, Peter! No! See! You don't understand a damn word that I'm saying to you! Look. Snooks is going to get a screwed-up book because he's colored, but you are also going to get a screwed-up book because you are going to be one of the poor white kids in the school. So you don't have to give Snooks your book, because both of the books will be screwed-up. Now, do you understand me?"

"Yes," replied Peter. "But I'm not going to school, Sister."

"You have to go to school, Peter. That's why Mom had you vaccinated by Doctor Amos last month."

"I'm still not going to school, Sister. If someone hits me or Snooks, I'll start crying! So will Snooks!"

"You and Snooks can't cry, Peter, because if you do, the other kids will keep picking on you and Snooks." Connie's facial expression was so intense, her voice so insistent that Peter had no choice but to listen to what she was saying to him. "You have to learn to tell them to go pound salt! And don't worry about your first year at school, because me and Jimmy Bobjack will be watching out for you and Snooks."

"You told me that...already, Sister," Peter said hesitantly to Connie.

She went on, ignoring his comment. "No one will bother you two with us around. But once me and Jimmy Bobjack move on to Ben Franklin, you and Snooks are going to be on your own, and you have to learn how to fist fight.

"I'm not going to hit anybody!" Peter hollered.

"You have to learn how to fight, Peter! If you can't protect yourself, then the other kids will start to pick on you, especially if they know you won't fight back!"

"No! I won't hit anybody!"

"And why not?" Connie demanded. "I'll teach you how to fight!"

"No, Sister! No!"

Connie frowned at her brother, then, deliberately, she changed from her demanding attitude to one of concern. "Look, Peter. You have to learn how to fight so you can protect yourself and Snooks. It's not hard. I'll teach you."

"No! I saw Dad hitting Mom, and Mom cried! She had a black eye, and blood was coming out of her mouth, Sister! I'll never hit anybody! I'm afraid of people getting hurt!"

"Well, you'll be more than afraid if you don't learn how to fight. What Dad did to Mom is a different situation. You see, Peter, Dad was drunk, and he didn't know what he was doing when he hit Mom."

"But Mom was crying! And she had blood all over her!" Peter looked suddenly like he, himself, had just been hit as he said this to Connie. "Didn't you ever see the blood, Sister?"

"Yes, Peter," Connie responded quietly to her brother, "I saw the blood." Her voice trailed off as she said the word 'blood'. Then she snapped herself back to the situation at hand. She heard Peter speak.

"I don't care if they hit me at school, Sister, I won't hit them back. I'll run and get you and Jimmy Bobjack if anybody picks on me and Snooks at the school."

"I'm not talking about Lincoln, Peter. I'm talking about when I go to Franklin." Connie's exasperation was beginning to show in her voice as well as in her gestures.

"Snooks and me can go to the big school with you and Jimmy Bobjack after the first grade."

"Now listen to me, Peter," Connie insisted. "You have to go six years to the grade school at Lincoln before you are able to go to junior high school. Look, we'll go over this again tomorrow. Do you know how to count numbers?"

"Yes, Miss Willie and Mr. Hawkins teach me how to

count when I go over to their house."

"What about your letters?"

"I get them all mixed up, Sister."

"Who helps you on the letters?"

"Miss Willie, Sister."

"No wonder you're mixed up!" said Connie.

Peter and Connie sat quietly together for a few moments on the river bank. Suddenly, Peter leaned over and kissed Connie on the cheek. "That's it, Peter!" Connie shouted. "Act like a goddamn sissy, so that the likes of Patty Ann Johnson can beat the living shit out of you!"

"I love you, Sister," Peter said as he put his arms around Connie.

Connie was embarrassed, but she could not resist her little brother's affection. She hugged him back. "I love you too, Peter."

"And you love Mom, Sister," Peter asked, holding on to Connie.

"Of course I love Mom! What a stupid question!"

"And Miss Willie and Mr. Hawkins? Do you love them, Sister?"

"Yes, Peter. I love Miss Willie and Mr. Hawkins," Connie replied, her eyes moist.

And so with the summer of 1947 coming to an end, and Mrs. Vitello no longer with the Di Santangelo family, Peter never went back to Mr. Bump's farm. Instead, he went with Augustina and Connie to the tin mill every day to sell the large baskets of baked bread, pizza slices, and Mother's Oats oatmeal cookies. While Augustina would stand at the main entrance to the tin mill, Connie and Peter would go to the rear opening, near the shipping dock, where Peter would hold the basket of goods, and Connie would yell at the top of her voice to the tin mill workers, "GET YOUR MOTHER SOME MOTHER OATMEAL COOKIES, MOTHERS!"

And when Augustina went down to the center of New Castle in her blue and white polka dot dress to apply for work, Peter would stay with Willie Hawkins and work diligently on his numbers and letters. He would listen to Miss Willie reading the Bible, while Connie and Jimmy Bobjack Hunter would sneak over to old man Thompson's garage to smoke.

And in these ways, the family waited out the final days of summer for the beginning of Peter Di Santangelo's first year of school.

XI

It was invariable and uniform. It was bound to happen; the only thing in doubt was the specific event at a specific time. It was very evident among the black people of the neighborhood, who were addicted to drinking too much liquor.

Many times, sitting around the dinner table, Dabney Hawkins would say to Willie Hawkins, and the Di Santangelos, that when you take a man and take his pride away, you have to eventually kill the man inside. And it didn't matter how you do it; drinking or driving him away from his family. You are bound to destroy the man.

The majority of the black families of the isolated neighborhood knew what awaited their male children as they reached the age of discretion. And because of this situation, the black people of the neighborhood concentrated on grooming and educating the female members of the family, in hope that they would at least be able to get respectable employment as typists or secretaries at the tin mill or in the business district of New Castle. Occasionally, one of the black men would be hired to work the intensely heated area by the raging furnaces of the tin mill, to produce the silvery metallic elements from the furnaces.

And this existence was not restricted to the black men of the tin mill. Many of the white men who performed various mill functions would enter and depart the neighborhood by way of the viaduct, and by the end of a normal work shift were hardly recognizable because of the filthy conditions they were subjected to in the plant. But the workers were deprived of education, and because of this, went into the tin mill to work, spitting out the dust and dirt from their guts, in order to save money for the education of their own children.

Perhaps if Peter's maternal grandfather, Giuseppe Vitello, had lived, instead of dying on the floor of the tin mill in 1925 at the age of fifty-four, the family's lives could have been different.

Peter was too young to know why his father drank so much; why he so violently mistreated Peter and

Peter's mother, Augustina, whom Peter loved so very much.

And so it happened, for the specific time came at which it was bound to happen. It was Monday, August 25th, exactly two months after Peter's sixth birthday. After completing her Monday wash and their noon trip to the tin mill, Augustina went into downtown New Castle to put in more job applications.

Peter stayed with Willie Hawkins all afternoon, since Augustina was not due back until shortly after four o'clock. Willie Hawkins was very busy working as a laundress on Mondays. And at nearly four o'clock in the afternoon, Peter had grown tired of watching Willie Hawkins do the FitzSimons' laundry. He had watched his mother working at the wringer washer during the entire morning at his home.

He thought about the cigar box Dabney Hawkins had given him one day to keep his baseball cards in because Connie had a tendency to increase her collection at Peter's expense. Peter did not have many cards in his box, thanks to his sister, but what cards he had, he spent many hours flipping with Snooks to see how many of them would land face up on the ground. Connie had become the hottest card flipper in the neighborhood as was very obvious from the stacks of cards on her dresser. And although Peter was sure some of those were actually his, he had orders from Connie never to go near the cards on her dresser, if he had any desire to live long enough to start school.

Augustina had always instructed Peter that he was never to go near their own house when she had left him in the care of Willie Hawkins.

Peter knew that there was no way of knowing when his father would come home. Since, often, his father would leave or miss work entirely and go to the social clubs in Mahoningtown where he would drink himself senseless. He would then be thrown out of the clubs and come home.

Peter was never a disrespectful child, because he sensed that what his mother said to him was for his own protection. He had seen his mother many mornings with a black eye and swollen face. And often, in the past when Peter began to hear his father calling his mother names, and hitting her repeatedly, he would silently cry and huddle his small, trembling body against his grandmother's in bed. He would lie there almost entirely hidden except for the very top of his small, dark-haired head which lay on the pillow barely showing above the blanket top.

His grandmother would hold him gently and stroke his head to ease the trembling. And she would sing softly to him in Italian until the abusive noises of shouting and hitting eventually stopped. And often, in the past after his father had battered his mother, Mr. Di Santangelo would aggressively lunge into the second bedroom and forcefully remove Peter from Mrs. Vitello's bed. Taking possession of Peter, his father, raging angrily, would ferociously plunge Peter down the stairwell into the kitchen, where Mr. Di Santangelo would grab a kitchen chair and take it and Peter down into the cellar of the house. Mr. Di Santangelo would sit Peter on the chair and hog-tie him with Augustina's clothesline, leaving Peter in the darkness of the earth covered cellar floor.

In time, Mrs. Vitello would get out of bed and in her stockingless feet and her kimono, homemade from a discarded bed spread, would edge her way, skillfully manipulating the walls with her hands, down the stairwell, navigate through the kitchen, and down into the darkened cellar. "Petro? Petro?" she would softly sing out to Peter.

Peter, crying, would whisper back in Italian for his grandmother to be careful so that she did not fall down the steps. When Mrs. Vitello finished her tactical journey of trudging legwork and rigorous handwork, she would reach the cellar and maneuver her way toward Peter. When Mrs. Vitello reached Peter she would billow the chair to the ground so that Peter's head rested on the back of the chair, the rest of his rope bounded body would sit on the lower part of the chair. Mrs. Vitello would then kneel down, raise the back of the chair and, while gliding her legs under it, gently rested the chair on her lap. Peter would continue crying as he listened to his grandmother tell him how much he looked like his grandfather, Guiseppe, and about their train ride on the roof of a passenger train from New York to New Castle.

In time Peter would eventually fall asleep as his grandmother continued her stories about her youth and her beloved husband. As Peter slept, Mrs. Vitello would remove her beads from the pocket of her kimono and recite the rosary, oblivious to the rats on the move around the upper part of the old cement stone walls of the cellar.

In the morning Augustina, her eyes battered black and blue, her protruding lips blistered and clotted with withered blood, would find her way to the cellar, re-move the chair from her mother's lap, straighten the chair and unbind Peter. Augustina would then break down from exhaustion and, in defeat, collapse on the earth covered ground, crying, asking her mother and her son to forgive her. Peter and his grandmother would lift Augustina to her feet as the three of them would cry, hug and kiss each other. They would then mount the cellar steps, Augustina in front holding Peter's hand behind her, Mrs. Vitello behind Peter with her hand on his right shoulder, toward the kitchen, where Augustina would prepare breakfast for Peter and his grandmother before their trip to Mr. Bump's farm.

Wearying of the dull afternoon with Willie Hawkins, Peter went over to the Di Santangelo house to get the cigar box. He intended to take it back to the Hawkins house and flip the baseball cards on the porch until his mother came home from her interviews. He walked into the kitchen, closed the door behind him, and went up the stairs to his bedroom, which he shared with Connie.

After getting the cigar box from underneath his bed, Peter looked inside to assure himself that Connie had not taken any recent liberties with his cards. Then he hurried down the stairs and into the kitchen toward the door. As he reached for the door knob, he noticed that it was already turning. He pulled his hand away from the doorknob and stood perfectly still, staring at the slowly turning knob. He took another step away from the door and glanced up, expecting to see his mother come through the door. He knew she would be upset that he had come home alone to his house.

As Peter was getting ready to explain to his mother why he had come home alone, he was suddenly aware that it was not his mother who was entering the house, but his father. Even before he saw who it was, Peter knew that it was his father for the awful stench of his whiskey preceded him.

"Well, well, well," Samuel Di Santangelo said, his speech slurred as he gently swayed back and forth. He looked around the kitchen for Augustina, and seeing that she was not in sight, he looked back at Peter.

Peter's glance darted around the room, then he moved quickly away from Samuel Di Santangelo toward the kitchen table. His father entered the kitchen, slammed the kitchen door behind himself, and snapped the lock.

"Where's that whore, your mother?"

Peter moved closer to the table, shaking from chills of fear. He started to cry.

"Is that bitch upstairs, boy?"

Peter did not answer. He continued to move back until he felt the edge of the kitchen table against his upper back.

Samuel Di Santangelo yelled harshly. "Get the fuck over here!"

As his father came closer, Peter edged around the table, dropping the cigar box onto the floor. Then he plunged under the round, wooden kitchen table.

Samuel Di Santangelo grabbed Mrs. Vitello's large pasta rolling stick near the kitchen cupboards and started to swing it under the table, forcing Peter to scramble out and run to the kitchen door. Samuel Di Santangelo's drunkenness threw him off balance as Peter wrenched at the door knob, but the kitchen door was locked.

Peter turned around and saw his father coming toward him. He ran toward the steps and up the stairs leading to his bedroom, breathing quickly as he ran. When he reached the top of the stairwell, he looked down and saw his father coming up the stairs, trying to keep his balance, and gripping the pasta stick tightly in his right hand.

Peter ran into his bedroom, slammed the door, and jumped to the window searching desperately for his mother. Augustina was nowhere to be seen. Peter heard the hollow sound of his father's footsteps outside the door. Terrified, the little boy kept his eyes glued to the brown, wooden door knob. Slowly, the knob turned. The door, which had no lock, opened easily. Samuel Di Santangelo's sturdy, frame filled the doorway. His father's body swayed as he took an even firmer grip on the pasta stick, never taking his eyes from Peter as he did so.

Peter stood, crying and trembling, with his back to the window. His arms hung loosely at his sides. Nervously, he clenched and unclenched his hands. His hazel-green eyes widened. He swallowed hard and the solitary little boy cried out, "No, Dad." His father advanced, slowly, like an animal stalking its prey. He carried the heavy pasta stick out in front. Peter dived for the large bed he had shared with his grandmother, and quickly slid under it. The frightened child never lost sight of the lethal stick as Samuel Di Santangelo, in a drunken rage, thrust it back and forth under the bed, trying to force Peter out.

"Come out from under there, you little son-of-a-bitch!" Samuel Di Santangelo yelled, kneeling at the side of the large double bed, swinging the pasta rolling stick underneath.

Peter kept moving under the bed, dodging the stick, which occasionally found its target. And then Peter heard his mother pounding frantically on the kitchen door, screaming, "Peter! Peter!"

Trapped under the bed, Peter tried but could not escape as Samuel Di Santangelo doubled his efforts to drive him out. Finally, from downstairs came the sound of glass shattering. Peter knew that what he had heard was the kitchen porch window breaking, and that his mother was trying to break into the locked house. As he heard the glass crashing, Samuel Di Santangelo lost his balance and fell into the bed. In that instant, the alert little boy darted from beneath the bed and ran as fast as his legs could carry him to the stairwell, down the steps and into the kitchen.

Samuel Di Santangelo ran behind his son, down the steps, muttering unintelligibly under his breath. He still carried the pasta stick.

When Peter got to the kitchen, Augustina grabbed him and shoved him toward the door. She unlocked the spring and bolt and pulled the door open almost in one movement. "Run, Peter!" she cried out. "Run over to Miss Willie's!"

Samuel Di Santangelo lurched into the kitchen from the stairwell, and before Augustina was able to realize what was happening, Samuel Di Santangelo came down on top of her with a loud outcry. "Augustina! Augustina, the whore!" he shouted repeatedly, pushing her around ruthlessly. Never did he lose his grip on the pasta stick. "And who did we fuck today, whore?" he cried, slamming Augustina up against the kitchen table.

"Sam! Please!" Augustina cried out, and then she shouted to Peter. "Run, Peter, Run!"

Samuel Di Santangelo doubled up his fist and punched Augustina sharply in the mouth several times. Peter stared at his parents, flinching as each blow fell. He saw blood appear on his mother's face.

Samuel Di Santangelo hit her mightily again, knocking her to the floor. He could barely hold his balance as he hit Augustina again and again and again. "Whore! Whore! Whore!" he shouted. And there followed upon each name the sickening thud of a heavy-fisted blow to the face of Augustina. Augustina flung her arms helplessly over her bloody face. She called out to Peter again and again. But, as she grew inevitably weaker, the sound of her voice calling, "Run, Peter! Run!" grew more and more faint. So that, finally, Peter could barely hear her as she begged him to save himself.

Suddenly, Peter dashed back toward his mother. Samuel Di Santangelo saw him coming, out of the corner of his eye. He took aim and swung the pasta stick at his child. This time he hit Peter hard on his shoulder, knocking the slight six-year old boy hard against the wringer-washer.

With Peter out of the way, at least for the moment, Samuel Di Santangelo turned the force of his warped, drunken attention back toward Augustina. "And who did you take care of today, you goddamn fucking whore!" He raised the stick over his head and gripping it with both hands, brought the full force of his weapon down on Augustina's shuddering body. "Answer me, goddamn it!" he screamed viciously. "Whose fucking cocks were in you today, whore!"

As Augustina lowered her arms to protect her breasts, Samuel Di Santangelo swung the stick against her head. He brought the pasta stick swiftly down upon the top of her head, and with each crushing blow, he cried out, "Whore! Whore! Whore!" He beat her relentlessly with the stick so that ultimately Augustina's blood-covered face was not recognizable.

Peter, crying and lying motionless next to the wringer-washer, was transfixed by the white polka dots on his mother's blue dress as slowly, slowly they turned from white to pale pink to blood red. Pitifully, his young voice was heard above the chaos crying out, "Mom! Mom!"

Samuel Di Santangelo continued his brutal assault, delivering one savage blow, then another and another all over Augustina's body. Finally, he came down with all of his might on her head, one - two - three times as the horrible sound of bone being crushed accompanied each lethal blow of the pasta stick to Augustina's head.

The smashing of the porch window, the recurrent

thunder of Samuel Di Santangelo's shouting, and the terrified screams of Augustina brought Willie Hawkins running, in terror, to the house. She was followed by Connie. Miss Willie and Connie were struck silent when they saw Augustina lying in a pool of her own blood. They looked from the body on the floor to the loathsome figure of Samuel Di Santangelo standing remorselessly over the body of the pathetic woman who was his wife.

"Miss Augustina! Miss Augustina!" screamed Willie Hawkins in anguish. She stood near the kitchen sink, next to the door. She turned mechanically to the silverware drawer, then in angry desperation, she snatched up a knife. Her typically gentle face contorted fearfully. She took a step toward Samuel Di Santangelo. Her eyes grew more and more menacing as she placed one foot in front of the other.

Suddenly, she screamed at him. "Get out of here, Mr. Sam, get out of here!" She repeated her command several more times, never taking her eyes from him.

Connie, standing by the refrigerator, let out two long, piercing screams. Then she fell completely silent and stared, unseeing, at her mother.

Samuel Di Santangelo watched Willie Hawkins as she came closer and closer to him, the knife blade thrust forward as she walked.

"You better get the fuck out of here!" he yelled at Willie Hawkins. "You don't belong in this fucking house!"

Willie Hawkins advanced closer and closer to Samuel Di Santangelo and holding the knife steadily, she shouted, "No, Mr. Sam! You best just turn around and walk out of here, before I run this knife into you!"

Samuel Di Santangelo, swaying back and forth, kept looking at Willie Hawkins. He turned around and looked down at Augustina lying on the bloody floor.

Willie Hawkins, still advancing, was by now just a few feet away from Samuel Di Santangelo. "Get out of here! So help me, Mr. Sam, as God is my witness, I'll shove this knife into you, if you don't get the hell out of here right now!"

Samuel Di Santangelo dropped the pasta stick and backed toward the kitchen door. Willie Hawkins kept flashing the knife. Connie stood frozen against the re-frigerator, her eyes fixed on her mother while, Peter lay, unmoving, next to the wringer-washer, looking at what was happening between Miss Willie and his fa-ther.

Samuel Di Santangelo braced himself against the kitchen sink and looked down at Augustina's bloody body. He looked at Willie Hawkins, with tears in his eyes.

"I'm no fucking good. *No fucking good for listening and believing everybody's lie since I was young!*" He turned toward the kitchen door and walked slowly out of the house. And as he went, Samuel Di Santangelo did not look back.

Willie Hawkins went over to Augustina and knelt down beside her. "Miss Augustina?" she called in a whisper. "Miss Augustina?" There was no response. She turned to Connie. "Go over to my place and get Mr. Hawkins, child!" she shouted softly to Connie. "And if he isn't there, child, run down to Mr. Adam's beer Garden to fetch him!"

Connie did not budge from where she stood. She did not react in any way to Willie Hawkins. She stood motionless and stared, at the still body of her mother.

"Child!" shouted Willie Hawkins. "I said to go and fetch Samuel Hawkins!"

But, Connie was not able to move, nor was she able to hear the voice of Willie Hawkins or to understand her words. Connie was capable of one thing and of one thing only and that was to stand in one spot and stare, transfixed, at her mother.

Willie Hawkins ran over to Connie and slapped her face. "Child?" When Connie did not move, Willie Hawkins slapped her again. "Child?" She left Connie and ran to the kitchen door from where she shouted for her father. "Mr. Hawkins! Mr. Hawkins!"

Dabney Hawkins, who had just returned from the FitzSimons' estate and still had on his working clothes, came running over to the Di Santangelo house. He looked inside the kitchen and saw Augustina, with Willie Hawkins kneeling over her. He went over to them.

"Oh, my God!" he said as he grabbed Willie Hawkins. Mr. Sam! Goddamn you, Mr. Sam!"

"Mr. Sam was in here drunk, Mr. Hawkins!" Willie Hawkins said with fear, disbelief and hatred in her eyes.

Dabney Hawkins took the knife out of Willie Hawkins' hand and took it over to the sink. "Let's get the children out of here," he said to Willie Hawkins.

"The girl won't move, Mr. Hawkins. She's sort of acting dumb like."

Dabney Hawkins ran over to Connie. "Connie?" he called to her as he shook her shoulder. He stood right in front of her, knees bent and shoulders hunched a bit so that he could look right into her eyes. Again he called to her, "Connie?" He called a little louder and got no response.

"I told you, Mr. Hawkins, the child won't move!"

He straightened up and turned toward Peter who was by now huddled against the wringer-washer, where he had been thrown earlier by his father. Peter's slight arms were folded tightly across his chest. The little boy's lips were parted as though he wanted to but could not call out or speak. His wide-open eyes reflected the terror and horror of what he had just seen. He trembled.

"What about Sugar?" Dabney Hawkins asked as he turned toward Peter.

Willie Hawkins rushed toward Peter. When she saw him, she cried, "Sugar? Are you all right, Sugar?"

Peter tried visibly to stop shaking. He looked at

Willie Hawkins and replied, "Yes, Miss Willie. I'm all right. My dad hit mom with Mamo's macaroni stick! He wouldn't stop hitting her, Miss Willie. Mr. Hawkins, he just kept hitting her and I...."

"Stop your shaking, Sugar," she said quietly to the little dark-haired boy. She got down on the floor and held him for just a moment to ease his trembling. "There isn't anyone going to hurt you," Willie Hawkins said as she picked Peter up from the kitchen floor. "Can you walk, Sugar?"

Peter nodded his head and kept his gaze fixed on his mother, lying on the kitchen floor.

"You take Sugar, Miss Willie," Dabney Hawkins said. I can carry the girl out of here."

"Where are we going to take them?" Willie Hawkins asked.

"We'll take them over to the Salvation Army head-quarters before Mr. Sam comes back looking for them."

Dabney Hawkins picked up Connie and carried her in his arms; her eyes were still fixed, glassily, on her mother. Peter clung onto Willie Hawkin's hand as they walked out of the house and headed for the Hawkins' yard.

"You better go down to Mr. Tom's and tell Mr. Tom and Miss Libby what happened and to call the police and Dr. Amos, Miss Willie," Dabney Hawkins said. "And tell them to to get over here right away!" He looked at Peter. "You come over here, Sugar, and stand by Mr.

Hawkins until Miss Willie gets back."

Peter and Dabney Hawkins stood side by side in the yard until Willie Hawkins came running back from Mr. Tom's store. "I told Mr. Tom and Miss Libby what happened. Mr. Tom and Miss Libby are coming over here to watch the house until the policemen and Dr. Amos come for Miss Augustina."

"Good," Dabney Hawkins said. "Now let's get the hell out of here. And if any of the white folks try to stop us, after we cross the viaduct, and ask what we are doing with the white children, you just start running, Miss Willie. You understand?"

"Yes, Mr. Hawkins," Willie Hawkins answered. "I understand."

And so they left the Hawkins' yard, Willie Hawkins holding the hand of Peter, whose legs were so short that he could hardly keep up with her, and Dabney Hawkins, struggling under the dead weight of carrying the eleven year old Connie.

The four of them went over the viaduct to Moravia Street, and headed for the center of New Castle. When they arrived at the Salvation Army headquarters near the Diamond Square, Willie Hawkins pounded on the entrance door with her fist.

"Mrs. Major! Mrs. Major!" Willie Hawkins shouted.

Through the large plate window, Willie and Dabney Hawkins could see Mrs. Major Hoffman running to the front door.

XII

The next morning, Mrs. Major Hoffman went to one of the small bedrooms at the rear of the headquarters to get Peter. She found him sitting on the edge of the bed, fully dressed in the clothes he had worn to the headquarters the night before. And except for his shirt which was buttoned crookedly and one shoe whose laces were untied, he looked like any little boy who had dressed himself for any normal day.

"May I fix your shirt, Peter?" Mrs. Major Hoffman asked.

"Yes, thank you," said Peter, looking down at the older woman's fingers as she rebuttoned his shirt. She then knelt down and tied his shoe laces. They left the room and began to walk down the long hall which led to Mrs. Major Hoffman's office. As he walked by her side, Peter looked up at Mrs. Major Hoffman tentatively then reached up and took her hand.

Mrs. Major Hoffman showed Peter to a chair then she took a seat at her oak roll-top desk.

"Peter," said Mrs. Major Hoffman, "I want to talk to you."

" Where is Sister, Mrs. Major?" Peter asked politely. "Connie is still asleep in the other bedroom," Mrs. Major Hoffman replied, as she smiled kindly. "Your sister will be staying with us for a few days, Peter. She's asleep now, and we will take good care of her for you. Are you ready for breakfast, Peter?"

Peter sat on a large wooden chair next to the roll-top desk. "Mom always gives me oatmeal to eat in the morning." He became excited. "Mrs. Major! My dad hit my mom, and he hurt her!"

"You mustn't think about last night, Peter," Mrs. Major Hoffman said.

"Is my mom here?"

"No, she's not, Peter.

"Is mom with Miss Willie and Mr. Hawkins?"

"I don't think so, Peter."

"There was blood all over the floor, Mrs. Major!" said Peter. He had been sitting up quite straight in the wooden chair, one hand on either arm of the chair, gripping each chair arm tightly.

As he said these last words, he leaned forward and spoke so earnestly to Mrs. Major Hoffman that she was quietly shaken. She collected herself quickly and said, "Please don't think about what happened yesterday, Peter. About breakfast. I don't believe we have any hot oatmeal cereal here at the headquarters, but we do have corn flakes. Do you like corn flakes, Peter?"

"I don't know what it is, Mrs. Major. Mom always gives me the oatmeal when I get up."

"Yes, I know, Peter. But corn flakes are very good. Would you eat a bowl of cereal for me?"

"Yes, thank you, Mrs. Major."

"Before you eat, Peter, I would like to ask you a few questions. Have you ever been on a large bus before, Peter?"

"Yes. We went to work with Miss Willie and Mr. Hawkins on a bus. And we went with Mamo to the park on the bus."

"You're talking about one of the city buses, Peter."

"It was a real big bus, Mrs. Major!"

"Very good, Peter," Mrs. Major Hoffman said. "Now I am going to tell you about a very, very large bus. And this is a surprise for you, Peter! After you have breakfast, I am going to put you on a large bus, and you are going to go for a very long ride, which you will just love! And you are going to go to a nice place called Philadelphia. Have you ever heard of a place called

Philadelphia?"

"Is it where Miss Willie and Mr. Hawkins live?"

"No, Peter. It is a long, long way off from here, and a very long, long ride on the large bus I'm telling you about."

"Is Sister coming with me on the bus?"

"No, Peter. I have already told you that Connie will have to stay with us for a little while. But there will be many people on the bus for you to talk with on the trip to Philadelphia."

Peter had settled back in his chair but, once again, he leaned forward and came very close to speak more intensely to Mrs. Major Hoffman. "Sister has to come with me, Mrs. Major! I'll take care of her, Mrs. Major. I cannot go without Sister. Sister and Jimmy Bobjack would worry about me, Mrs. Major. You see, Sister loves me very much. I have to take her with me, Mrs. Major." Having said this he heaved a huge sigh and then settled back once more in the chair with the wooden arms, still holding onto the chair arms. His feet in their black clodhoppers dangled a foot away from the floor.

"I have no doubt that you would, Peter," Mrs. Major Hoffman said, putting her hand on Peter's head. "But you will have to let me take care of Connie for you."

"Is my mom going with me?"

Mrs. Major Hoffman removed her hand from Peter's head and took his hand in hers. "Peter, listen to me carefully. You are going to be by yourself on the large bus. But, you must remember that there will be a lot of people on the bus. And when you get to Philadelphia, someone from the Salvation Army will meet you at the bus station in Philadelphia."

"Are you going to be on the bus, Mrs. Major?"

"No, Peter, but when you arrive in Philadelphia, the lady from the Salvation Army will be wearing the same type of uniform that I have on. So, I will really be there, Peter, but it will be another lady that is dressed like me."

"I'm not going without Sister or my mom, Mrs. Major! You don't know what happened! My dad hit my mom, and she had blood all over her," Peter said excitedly.

"I do know what happened last evening, Peter. Miss Willie told me all about it. Now, why don't we have a small bite to eat. We'll have some corn flakes, and then we can talk a little bit about the bus ride to Philadelphia." She smiled, as she looked at Peter. "Oh, Peter, you have no idea how big this bus is!"

"Is it a fast bus, Mrs. Major?" Peter asked.

After breakfast, Mrs. Major Hoffman took Peter to the Greyhound Bus Depot on Jefferson Street, about three blocks from the Army Headquarters. When they arrived, Willie Hawkins and Dabney Hawkins were waiting for them outside the depot.

"Miss Willie!" Peter yelled.

"Sugar!" Willie Hawkins yelled back. She rushed

over to Peter, then bent down and put her arms around him. "Are you all right, Sugar?" she asked.

"He is fine," Mrs. Major Hoffman answered.

Willie Hawkins stood up and looked at Mrs. Major Hoffman. "Where is the girl? You didn't say anything about—"

"She is at the Headquarters," Mrs. Major Hoffman intruded. "I will tell you later. Please stay here with Peter while I go inside the station and make arrangements for him."

Willie Hawkins held Peter's hand while they waited for Mrs. Major Hoffman to return. "Where is the Mrs. Major Hoffman sending you, Sugar?"

"On a big bus," Peter replied.

Dabney Hawkins became visibly upset. He put his arm on Peter's shoulder and asked him, "Where are you going on this big bus, Sugar?"

"I don't know Mr. Hawkins but Mrs. Major says that my mom and Sister can't come with me."

"Didn't the Mrs. Major tell you where this big bus was going?" Dabney Hawkins asked.

"Yes, Mr. Hawkins." Peter answered.

"Where, Sugar?"

"I can't remember. It was a big word that Mrs. Major told me."

When Mrs. Major Hoffman returned, she explained to Willie Hawkins and Dabney Hawkins that the Philadelphia headquarters was to handle Peter's case, considering the circumstances.

"Is anyone going to go with Sugar on the bus, Mrs. Major Hoffman," Dabney Hawkins asked.

"We are understaffed, and we just don't have the personnel at the headquarters to travel, Mr. Hawkins. Peter will have someone from the Army headquarters meet him at the bus station in Philadelphia. The bus driver will be given full responsibility for Peter's safe conduct to Philadelphia." She smiled reassuringly at Dabney and his daughter. "Please be assured that Peter will be well taken care of. This is the way we always handle such cases. When Peter arrives in Philadelphia, everything will be new for him. He won't have anyone there to remind him of New Castle. Please try to understand."

"But, the other child, Mrs. Major?" asked Willie Hawkins. "What about the girl?"

"You may return to the headquarters with me after we see Peter on his way. I will explain everything to you at the Army headquarters."

They waited for the Greyhound bus for Philadelphia. Willie Hawkins stood there at the bus depot in New Castle, Pennsylvania and held the hand of this little six year old boy. And in that tiny gesture lay the deep love she felt for her dearest friend, Augustina, who was now dead and for the children of her friend.

Dabney Hawkins, with his arm placed tenderly on Peter's shoulder, felt the same mixture of love and grief which his daughter was now feeling. But, from years of experience, he had learned how to hide what he felt and so his face remained fairly passive throughout the ordeal of saying good-bye to little Peter.

When the bus arrived, Dabney Hawkins pressed Peter to himself and gave him one final hug. "God Bless you, Sugar," he called out as Peter walked toward the bus holding onto Willie Hawkins' hand. Peter turned around and waved to Dabney Hawkins with his free hand. He did not say a word but it was not necessary for in that moment all that he felt for his friend, Dabney Hawkins, showed in the tenderness of his glance.

Willie Hawkins led Peter onto the bus and sat him down in the front seat. She opened the window to let in a little fresh air, and then looked at Mrs. Major Hoffman who stood outside of the bus talking to the driver.

"Now, Sugar, you have to listen to everything the mister that drives this bus tells you," Willie Hawkins said as she sat down next to Peter on the seat. "Do you hear Miss Willie, Sugar?"

"Yes, Miss Willie. I hear you."

"Miss Willie and Mr. Hawkins just want to be sure that you are going to be all right," Willie Hawkins said. She handed Peter a school box. "Miss Willie and Mr. Hawkins was saving this for you, Sugar. We were going to give this school box to you on your first day of school. It was sort of a little surprise for our Sugar."

Peter's attention began to wander as he heard somebody behind him cough. He turned around in his seat and in so doing looked away from Willie Hawkins briefly. Miss Willie called to him, "Sugar, do you hear me?"

Peter's glance returned quickly to Miss Willie and the school box.

Willie Hawkins continued. "This school box has everything in it that you will need for school, Sugar. Pencils, erasers, a pen, a little pair of scissors for cutting out pictures of Jesus, but you have to be very careful with them, Sugar, because they have sharp edges on them. And Miss Willie also put in two rainbow color note pads in the school box for you to print on. I even put in Miss Willie and Mr. Hawkins' home address on a piece of paper so you can write to Miss Willie and Mr. Hawkins when you do your learning at the school. The paper is taped to the inside bottom of the school box so you won't lose it. Are you hearing Miss Willie, Sugar?"

"Yes, Miss Willie," Peter answered. "Thank you for the school box. I don't know how to write, but I can draw. I can send you drawing pictures."

"You send me the drawing pictures, Sugar, and when you learn how to write at the school in Philadelphia, then you write Miss Willie and Mr. Hawkins and tell us all about the schooling. And I want you to promise to send Miss Willie cutouts of Jesus."

Dabney Hawkins and Mrs. Major Hoffman boarded the bus. Mrs. Major Hoffman put a name tag on Peter's shirt and instructed him to listen to the bus driver.

"Yes, Mrs. Major," Peter said. "I know because Miss Willie already told me to listen to the bus driver."

"Fine, Peter, but now listen to what I have to say to you," Mrs. Major Hoffman said. "When the bus pulls into a restaurant, you wait until the bus driver takes your hand and you stay with the bus driver, Peter, because the bus driver has the money for your lunch and your dinner, and when the bus arrives in Philadelphia you are to stay on the bus until everyone else is off the bus and wait for the bus driver to take you to a woman at the bus depot in Philadelphia who will be wearing the same type of uniform that I have on. Do you understand what I am saying to you, Peter?"

"Yes, Mrs. Major. I'll wait for the bus driver."

"You just listen to me, again. You stay on this bus and don't move from your seat until all of the people get off the bus, and then the bus driver will come over to your seat and he will get you. You are not to move until he comes for you. If you have to go to the rest room, you walk up to the driver and tell him that you have to go to the rest room."

"To pee?" Peter asked.

"Yes, Peter. But other than the rest room, there is no reason for you to leave your seat. Do you understand me, Peter?"

"Yes, Mrs. Major. I won't leave my seat."

When Mrs. Major Hoffman had finished speaking, Dabney Hawkins moved toward Peter and gave him the cigar box that Peter had dropped on the kitchen floor yesterday. He also gave him a box of animal crackers. He looked at Peter for a few seconds, and then gave him the second box of animal crackers that he was holding.

"You listen to what the Mrs. Major just said to you, Sugar," Dabney Hawkins said.

"Yes, Mr. Hawkins."

The passengers boarded the bus, then the bus driver took his seat. Willie Hawkins, Dabney Hawkins and Mrs. Major Hoffman got off the bus.

Peter looked frightened as his friends left. He clutched the cigar box, the animal crackers and the school box. Seeing in his rearview mirror that Peter was upset, the driver turned around and winked as he called to Peter, "All set, buddy?" Then he closed the door.

Willie Hawkins hurried over to stand by the window she had opened. "You mind what Mrs. Major Hoffman said to you, Sugar. You listen to the mister that drives this bus. Now, put your head out a little and let Miss Willie give you a big hug."

Peter leaned out the window and Willie Hawkins put her arms around him and kissed him. "Why are you shaking, Sugar? There isn't anyone that is going to hurt you."

"I'm afraid, Miss Willie," Peter said as he started to cry, clinging to Willie Hawkins' neck. "Please help me, Miss Willie."

"Oh, Sugar," Willie Hawkins said softly to Peter. "There is nothing to be afraid about. You just listen to the bus driver and everything is going to be all right. And Jesus is with you, Sugar, so you mustn't be afraid. Now, you stop your shaking, you hear?"

Dabney Hawkins came over to the window and put his arms around Peter and kissed him on the side of his face. "You be good, son," he said to Peter.

The bus started to move and Willie Hawkins started to walk alongside the bus. "Don't forget, Sugar, when you learn how to write you send Miss Willie one of those nice picture cards from Philadelphia. Are you hearing Miss Willie, Sugar?"

"Miss Willie!" Peter shouted, staring at Willie Hawkins as she walked by the side of the bus, talking to him through the window. "Don't you worry about nothing, Sugar. You are going to be all right. And you are going to like the schooling in Philadelphia where you are going, Sugar."

The greyhound bus started to pick up a little speed as it approached the Diamond Square and it became harder to understand what Willie Hawkins was saying. The wind caught some of her words as she called to Peter. "You grow up and be real smart just like Miss

Augustina would want you to be, Sugar." Willie Hawkins broke into a trot, with Dabney Hawkins running bravely right behind her.

"Remember, Sugar, no matter where you find yourself, Miss Augustina will be watching you from Heaven. You make Miss Augustina and Miss Willie real proud of our Sugar. Are you listening to Miss Willie, Sugar?" Willie Hawkins said, crying and trying to keep up with the Greyhound bus. "You be good, Sugar, and grow up by loving the people around you. You do that for Miss Augustina and Miss Willie, Sugar. Don't forget to write to Miss Willie and Mr. Hawkins, Sugar."

Dabney Hawkins, puffing, was right behind Willie Hawkins, echoing his daughter, "You write to us, Sugar. Soon as you learn how to write in school, you write to us. Miss Willie will read it to me, Sugar." Tears were flowing down the sides of his face. "And you be good for them folks in Philadelphia. Don't you be afraid, son, They'll take good care of you."

The bus turned at Diamond Square onto Washington Street, where it picked up full speed to head out of the city of New Castle.

Peter looked back and saw Willie Hawkins and Dabney Hawkins on the post-office street corner, waving, and he could barely hear them shouting, "Goodbye, Sugar. Take care of yourself for Miss Augustina and Miss Willie and Mr. Hawkins!"

Peter kept leaning out the window as the Greyhound

bus continued leaving the heart of the city. He could see Miss Willie and Mr. Hawkins waving to him and calling out to him. He shouted out the window, "Miss Willie! Mr. Hawkins!"

Finally, when he could no longer see Miss Willie and Mr. Hawkins, he sat down and folded his hands on his lap. He stared at the back of the driver's head. He looked down at the name tag on his shirt but he did not touch it. He listened to the powerful sound of the buses' motor when the driver shifted gears.

Peter sat there frightened and alone. He did not know why Miss Willie, Mr. Hawkins and Mrs. Major Hoffman had put him on the bus. He did not know where he was going or why he was going there. He did not understand what was happening to him. He did not know why his sister was not with him. He did not really understand what had happened to his mother. But, he remembered what Mrs. Major Hoffman had told him about not getting out of his seat. And so he sat there quietly.

After a little while, he opened the lid of the school box and looked inside of it. Then, he put it down and picked up the cigar box to see if Dabney Hawkins had gotten his baseball cards from the kitchen floor and put them inside. He noticed a hole had been punched through the lid of the cigar box, and when he opened the lid, he saw the cards inside with a gum band around them. Next to the cards, Dabney Hawkins had put his tiny radio, and next to the radio was the kitchen match box with Smitty in it. Peter smiled. He was happy that Mr. Hawkins had given him the radio, but he was especially happy to see Smitty sitting inside the box. He reached in and touched Smitty very gently on its back.

Peter put his cigar box on top of the school box and turned his attention toward the window next to the seat. He opened one of the boxes of animal crackers and started to eat them. And then he thought of what Dabney Hawkins had told him, and he turned and asked the bus driver if he had any cigarette butts, because he thought that Smitty might be hungry.

* * * * * * *

Dabney Hawkins' St. Louis Cardinals finished second to the Brooklyn Dodgers in the 1947 National League pennant race. And Connie's Detroit Tigers were very disappointing, coming in a poor second to the New York Yankees in the American League.

In October, the Yankees went on to defeat the Brooklyn "Bums," by four games to three, to take the 1947 World Series.

"You are my true and honorable wife,
As dear to me as are the ruddy drops
That visit my sad heart."

—*William Shakespeare   1599*
Julius Caesar, Act II

"Religion is a journey, not a destination."

—*Anonymous*

EPILOGUE

December 23, 1978

I

Walking over the viaduct, Peter could see that the black neighborhood had changed a lot. Public housing units now stood on both sides of the street. A multistory housing project loomed on the corner where Mr. Tom's general store had stood back in 1947.

Peter entered the Seven-to-Eleven store on the first level of the large building and asked where Willie Hawkins now lived.

No one was home at Willie Hawkin's unit. On the porch of the adjacent one, a large black woman appeared. "What do you want?" she asked Peter.

Peter smiled at the woman and said, "Hello. My

name is Peter Di Santangelo, and I'm looking for a Miss Willie Hawkins. The cashier over at the corner store told me that Willie Hawkins lives in this unit. I keep knocking but I don't think Miss Willie Hawkins is at home. Could you please tell me where I might be able to find her?"

The woman returned Peter's smile with a frown. "What do you want with Miss Willie Hawkins, mister?" she asked.

"I would like to talk to her. Will you please tell me where she is so that I may see her?"

Without answering, the woman went back into her unit. Peter walked to the front of the project unit and stood there, for he had decided it was best to wait for Willie Hawkins near the sidewalk. After a few minutes, a black man came out of the same unit the large, black woman had reentered. He walked up to Peter.

"My wife tells me you're looking for the Hawkins woman. What is it you want with Miss Willie Hawkins?" he asked as he stared with slight discomfort at Peter.

"I haven't seen Miss Willie Hawkins for a very long time, and I stopped to pay my respects to her."

"Are you with the welfare agency?" the black man questioned.

"No, sir," Peter answered. I used to live in this area when I was a child. Miss Willie Hawkins and her father, Mr. Dabney Hawkins, lived next door."

"I don't remember any white people ever living in

this neighborhood, and I've been living here a good many years, mister. A good fifteen years to be exact, and we have never had any white people in this section of the city." He looked suspiciously at Peter. "Are you with some sort of law enforcement agency?"

"No, sir," Peter replied. "I'm not with any law enforcement agency, and believe me, I am not with the welfare agency. My only desire is to see Miss Willie Hawkins and then I'll be on my way. I went over to the store in that multistory housing project right next to the viaduct and the counter woman directed me to this unit."

"Seeing that you say you're not with the welfare agency or with the law, who are you with that you want to see the Hawkin's woman?"

"I haven't seen Miss Willie Hawkins since the summer of 1947, that was when I left New Castle. I was driving through the city, today, and just stopped to say hello to her, sir."

Peter was becoming uncomfortable with the suspicion he was meeting with but he continued to speak politely and with respect. Peter glanced around the neighborhood, then pointed to the steel plant. "That steel mill used to be a tin mill back in the forties; and over there where those cars are parked, I used to live in a house that stood where that parking lot now stands. Miss Willie Hawkins and her father lived next door to us. When I left this neighborhood back in 1947, there was a small store owned by a black man and his wife, Mr. Tom and Miss Libby. It stood where that housing project now stands.

The black man was beginning to believe that Peter Di Santangelo was who he said he was but he was still uneasy with the idea of this white stranger's arrival in the neighborhood.

Then he relaxed a little. "Yes," he said, "that was the neighborhood back in the early sixties when we moved here. Miss Willie went down the ways a bit. I reckon she will be back soon, mister." He turned around and went back into his unit.

It started to snow as he stood there, thinking about the 1947 neighborhood. Everything had been torn down and replaced by the red brick and green boarded housing units, scattered all over the neighborhood. As the snow continued to fall, memories began to flood him. The feelings Peter had as he stood there thinking about his family, about his town and about his neighborhood were overwhelming. Except that the terrible helplessness he had felt as a boy was gone. In its place was a mixture of feelings; joy for the love he had known from his mother and sister, his grandmother and the Hawkinses, and deep sadness for the pain he had endured and which he had never understood.

Peter realized as he thought about these things that for him, the joy had far outweighed the pain. He had not fully realized until now that it was the love he had known that had nourished and sustained him.

Peter peered through the heavily falling snow and saw the hunched figure of an old black woman walking bravely against the bitter December wind. She tapped her cane silently as she walked past Peter and toward her unit. She did not look up at him.

Peter felt a sudden rush of tenderness. "Miss Willie," Peter called gently to her.

The old woman stopped quickly. She turned around and squinted through the snow at the stranger who was calling her name. Then she asked, "What is it you want with this old woman you call Miss Willie, sir?"

Peter tried hard to control his feelings. He asked in an awkward voice, "Are you Miss Willie Hawkins?"

The old woman stared questioningly at him.

"Miss Willie," Peter whispered. "I am Augustina Di Santangelo's son, Peter."

The old woman squinted hard at him from behind her bifocals. "It can't be," she said faintly. She tilted her head way back and looked vigilantly at Peter. "Sugar?"

The sound of Willie Hawkins calling him by that wonderful name which he had not heard for more than thirty years stunned Peter. He returned the old woman's stare.

"Sugar?" Willie Hawkins asked again, as she moved closer to Peter. "Oh, Lord, it can't be! Is it really you, Sugar? My Miss Augustina's Sugar?"

Peter went to her and hugged her. "Yes, Miss Willie.

It's Sugar."

"Oh, Sugar! Sugar!" Willie Hawkins cried out, hugging Peter. "Oh, Good, Good Almighty Lord! What the Holy Spirit has brought this woman for Christmas! I can't believe what this old woman has in front of her eyes!" She raised her head toward the sky, and she cried as she put her arms around Peter, "Amen, Jesus! Amen, my Good Lord!"

II

Peter sat in one of the two vinyl chairs at the small table, which was covered by a white cloth. He looked at the humble place in which Willie Hawkins lived, at the wooden napkin holder which held paper napkins, a glass salt and pepper shaker set, and a milky white plastic vase which held one artificial red rose. The simplicity of Willie Hawkin's home touched Peter.

He looked from the table to Willie Hawkins who stood near a small range, as she turned off the front burner under the coffee pot and then blew on the burner to assure that the flame was out.

It was not easy for Peter to recall Willie Hawkins'

size from so long ago but she seemed to be so much smaller than he remembered her. Perhaps it was the way she was so hunched over that made her appear so.

Willie Hawkins poured their coffee and sat down. "How long have you been waiting out there in the cold for Miss Willie, Sugar?"

"For a short while, Miss Willie," Peter answered as he took a sip of the hot coffee. "I believe I upset your neighbors. They had a hard time believing that I was a friend of the Hawkins' family and not someone from a law enforcement agency.

"The people in this neighborhood are not used to seeing any white people here, Sugar, excepting the mill workers coming through the neighborhood. But once in a while, one of the social workers comes over the viaduct to work in the project. But what brings you to New Castle, Sugar?"

"I was in Pittsburgh for a couple of days on business, I work for the government, Miss Willie, trying to help settle strikes between companies and unions."

"Are you living in Pittsburgh, Sugar? And are you married? You must tell Miss Willie everything about Sugar."

"I live in Buffalo, New York, Miss Willie. I moved there in 1969. That was the year I got married to a woman named Margaret." He smiled and took another sip of coffee. "I wish you could know her, Miss Willie. We met while I was in the army. I know you would like her. We have three children. The twins, Cathy and Teresa, are seven. Our son, Anthony was four years old on December 4th."

Willie Hawkins was especially surprised by the news of the twins. "Does Miss Margaret have a twin brother or sister, Sugar?" she asked.

"No," Peter answered, smiling. "We don't know why we had twins, Miss Willie. It doesn't run in Margaret's family." He continued, "I know so little about my people, Miss Willie."

"Oh, Sugar," Willie Hawkins said. "I only know the things that Miss Augustina told me and she never talked about her own people to me. My Miss Augustina worked so hard. We didn't really talk about family."

Peter looked disappointed but could tell when he saw the look on Willie Hawkins' face when she spoke the name of his mother, Augustina, that he was asking too much of the old woman.

He deliberately changed the subject and told Willie Hawkins all about Margaret's coming from Wyoming and of how each year they spent their vacations there with the children. He told her that Margaret's father was a rancher, a farmer, and that his children had been given a mare named Tessie and her colt named Montana and a dog named Cooper by their grandparents.

He spoke of his great admiration for farmers and at that Willie Hawkins' face lighted up. She said, "The Lord has never created a finer human person on His earth, Sugar, than the farmer."

Peter shook his head and agreed with her, "Yes, Miss Willie. Out of all the people I have met in my life, I believe that the farmer is the most honest and the most humble. There is no other group of people whom I respect as much as the farmers."

"They are the true Shepherds of the Lord's earth, Sugar," Willie Hawkins said, as she drank from the cup of coffee.

Peter and Willie Hawkins sat for some time in the little kitchen of her home. Peter recounted to her some of what went on in his life with Margaret and their children. Many times in the conversation he found his mind veering in a different direction from what they were speaking about. He felt a deep need to ask questions of Willie Hawkins concerning the family he had been a part of for the first six years of his life in New Castle.

Willie Hawkins recounted to Peter the story of the day some years before when she had gone into the city to get pills for her diabetes and how, when she was walking home, she took a wrong turn and ended up climbing the Highland Street hill which was in the opposite direction from her home. She knew then that she should not be walking to town alone anymore at the age of seventy-two.

Peter listened to her tale and realized as she talked about her daily life that she was expressing her own unspoken need not to speak of things from the past which would bring pain to herself and to Peter. And much as he needed to know about his family, his respect for Willie Hawkins' feelings and his own inborn sensitivity was greater than his need to know these things. And so the grown-up Peter sat as quietly in Willie Hawkin's kitchen and listened as attentively to his elder, as the little boy, Peter, would have listened so many years ago.

When Willie Hawkins had finished her story about getting lost on her way home from New Castle, Peter said, "I guess Mr. Hawkins is dead, Miss Willie."

"Oh, Good Lord, rest his soul. Mr. Hawkins died in 1960, Sugar. He had a heart attack working the grounds at the old FitzSimons' estate. Mr. Hawkins was dead before they found him, and Miss Willie has been by herself since then. Here, let me warm your coffee for you, Sugar."

"Do you remember the old neighborhood, Sugar?" she asked, as she returned to the table.

"Yes, I do, Miss Willie. I was thinking about the old neighborhood while I was waiting for you."

"But did you notice how it has changed?" she asked.

"It was very hard for me to recognize the place once I was over the viaduct," Peter replied. "I see that the old tin mill is still around, and they knocked down our old houses to make way for a parking lot."

"The old tin mill still stands, Sugar, but it's a steel

mill now. The people in the neighborhood tell me they make axles for cars and trucks in the plant now. Do you know what an axle is, Sugar?"

"Yes, Miss Willie. And I know all about the steel plant. I stopped at a service station when I arrived in New Castle, and when I mentioned the tin mill, the two men at the station had no idea what I was asking about until I mentioned the black neighborhood, and then one of the men explained to me that I was looking for the steel mill and not the tin mill."

Willie Hawkins got up every so often and walked to the range for the coffee pot. She and Peter talked quietly about the changes the city had made in the neighborhood: knocking down buildings, erecting a playground and a recreation hall. Willie Hawkins talked about going to the recreation hall every Friday night to play Bingo.

She spoke of Mr. Tom and Miss Libby. She asked Peter, "Do you remember Mr. Tom and Miss Libby?"

Peter replied, "I remember Mr. Tom because Snooks and I always used to go over to the store. Mr. Tom always gave us penny candy without charging us for it. I don't remember Miss Libby all too well. I can just barely picture her in my mind."

Suddenly, Peter leapt to a subject he had been avoiding since the beginning of their visit. "Miss Willie," he asked, "What happened to my sister, Connie?"

Willie Hawkin's face contorted painfully. "Oh, please,

Sugar. How I try to forget that day!" she said. "I am not the type to question the making and the doing of the Almighty, but He sure created an ugly day for us back then, Sugar. I have yet to see anything as ugly as that day that Satan walked through this neighborhood."

Peter had clearly seen the look on Willie Hawkin's face as she spoke of that "ugly day". And he would not have hurt her deliberately for anything but he needed so badly to know about his sister, Connie. "Do you know what happened to my sister, Miss. Willie?" Peter asked again.

Willie Hawkins looked directly at Peter. "Oh, Sugar," she said, "You remind me so much of my dear Miss Augustina." She put her hand to her face, removed her glasses and covered her eyes for a moment then she took her hand away and directed her gaze back to Peter.

"I have forgotten so much through all of these years, Sugar, and I really try not to think about that day." She lowered her eyes to the table and touched the coffee cup with her fingers. "It isn't any use talking about what happened so long ago, Sugar."

Peter was saddened to see that he was bringing so much pain to Willie Hawkins by asking her about his sister. He put his hand on top of Willie Hawkins' hand. "It's all right, Miss Willie," he said. "You don't have to worry about telling me what happened. Please believe me, Miss Willie."

"Oh, Sugar. Sugar. Why must we talk about what

happened. It is something in the past. It should be forgotten."

"I want to know what happened that night, Miss Willie. I want to know what happened to my sister, Connie."

Willie Hawkins sighed deeply and began. "When the Mrs. Major, the woman from the Salvation Army, put you on the bus for Philadelphia, the Mrs. Major told Miss Willie and Mr. Hawkins that they were going to send the child to some type of clinic."

"Did the Mrs. Major mention the name of the clinic, Miss Willie?"

"No, Sugar. I remember only that the Mrs. Major said a clinic. I don't recall that the Mrs. Major mentioned any name of a clinic. And if she did, but I am sure she didn't, Sugar, Miss Willie has forgotten, what with all of the years that have come and gone since that day of Satan. Mr. Hawkins and Miss Willie went back with the Mrs. Major to the Salvation Army headquarters after the bus had left, and they had the child in a room all by herself. She was sitting on a bed that was in the room. I remember how it hurt Miss Willie to see that child all alone there." Willie Hawkins looked tenderly at Peter. "Please, Sugar."

"You have nothing to worry about, Miss Willie. I assure you. I just want to know what happened to my family." Peter looked exhausted as he said this, as though the unanswered questions he had carried in his head for so many years were now draining him physically. He asked, "Did my sister say anything to you when you walked into the room?"

"When Mr. Hawkins and Miss Willie approached the child, the child acted as if she didn't know us. Mr. Hawkins tried to talk to the child, Sugar, but it wasn't any good of Mr. Hawkins to even have tried. The child just didn't know Mr. Hawkins or Miss Willie. Acted as if we were outsiders, Sugar. The Mrs. Major said that the child was not the same after she saw Miss Augustina on the floor, and all of the blood around Miss Augustina. You do know, Sugar, that Miss Augustina went to the Lord that day?"

"Yes, Miss Willie. I knew that my mother had died when I was in the orphanage in Philadelphia. As time went on, I realized that my mother had been killed."

Willie Hawkins lowered her head, and whispered, "Lord rest the soul of Miss Augustina." When she raised her head she said, "And that was the last time Miss Willie saw the child. And I never heard anything about the child since that day."

"Do you know what happened to my father, Miss Willie?"

Willie Hawkins looked at Peter. "You mean to tell me that after all of these years, Sugar, you still call Mr. Sam your father?"

"He is my father, Miss Willie. Nothing can ever change that. Did the police ever find my father?"

"No one really knows what happened to Mr. Sam, Sugar. Mr. Sam just sort of disappeared. Miss Willie knew that was going to happen, what with all that drinking and hitting Miss Augustina. Miss Willie and Mr. Hawkins always feared that something terrible was going to happen to either Miss Augustina or you, Sugar. Mr. Sam was an evil man, Sugar. He may have been your father, but Miss Willie saw the devil in Mr. Sam!"

"Are you telling me that no one knows what happened to my father after that day, Miss Willie?"

Suddenly, Peter got up from the table and began to walk back and forth in the tiny kitchen. He walked with his head down, his hands clasped behind his back, thinking. His brow was furrowed and for the first time since the beginning of his conversation with Willie Hawkins, he seemed to become agitated. Then after a minute or so, he regained his composure. He sat down and looked directly at Willie Hawkins as she spoke.

"There is no telling where he went after that day, Sugar. The police looked all over the city for Mr. Sam, especially down in the Mahoningtown section. But they never found Mr. Sam. Mr. Hawkins told me later that he thought Mr. Sam might of made it to the state border and headed out to another part of our country."

Peter sat nodding his head slightly, his lips tightly closed. It was as though the enormity of his father's having gotten away free stunned him as much as the hideousness of the murder he had committed. His next words, which he uttered without passion, were more a statement than a question. "Then no one saw him again?"

"Oh, Sugar, you know how people are at times. Mr. Tom told Mr. Hawkins shortly after that day, that Miss Libby told Mr. Tom that one of their shoppers saw someone peeping into Miss Augustina's house window one night, but I can't tell you if it was Mr. Sam or if it was a sneak thief or just one of the neighbors that was burning with curiosity. But Mr., Hawkins told Miss Willie that he didn't believe it was Mr. Sam."

As Peter talked with Willie Hawkins something seemed to go out of him. His manner became subdued and he appeared to grow weary. He continued to speak politely to her and to ask her the questions which had perhaps been haunting him on some level for most of his life.

Peter picked up the coffee pot and filled Willie Hawkin's cup and his own with the coffee. "And my mother, Miss Willie? I know that she died, but what happened to her after you and Mr. Hawkins took my sister and me to the Salvation Army?"

"Doctor Amos stopped over at our house after everything was over, and Doctor Amos told Mr. Hawkins and Miss Willie that Miss Augustina was dead before they got her to the hospital. Miss Willie and Mr. Hawkins went to the hospital to claim Miss Augustina, but the people at the hospital wouldn't release her to us, you know, Sugar, Mr. Hawkins and Miss Willie being colored people. Mr. Hawkins telephoned the Mrs. Major from Mr. Tom's store and the Mrs. Major agreed to go with us the following day to the hospital to get Miss Augustina, but the Mrs. Major said that she had to put you on that bus the first thing in the morning. That was why Mr. Hawkins and Miss Willie were at the bus station that morning, Sugar. After you were on your way to Philadelphia and we saw the child over at the Army headquarters, Mr. Hawkins, Miss Willie and the Mrs. Major left the Salvation Army and went to the hospital. The Mrs. Major signed the releasing papers, and then Miss Willie and Mr. Hawkins took Miss Augustina home in an ambulance. We buried Miss Augustina next to the Mrs. Mamo, Sugar, your grandmother. Mr. Hawkins and Mr. Tom took up another collection with the help of Miss Libby and we buried Miss Augustina the same way we buried the Mrs. Mamo, but we had to use our minister, Sugar, for the grave service. Mr. Hawkins said it would have been just useless to go and talk to the priest that came to the Mrs. Mamo's grave service."

Willie Hawkins got up and then went into the next room. She returned shortly with Augustina's prayer beads and Mrs. Vitello's white walking cane. She recounted to Peter the events of the morning after the murder of Augustina with so much detail that it seemed as though it might have all happened just three rather than nearly thirty years before. She told him of how Mrs. Major Hoffman had returned to the house and given the rosary beads to her, of how she and Mr. Hawkins had come back to the house and cleaned up the broken glass from the window, picked up the baseball cards and wiped Augustina's blood from the floor. It was then that Willie Hawkins had found the Mrs. Mamo's white cane near the sink.

As she handed the rosary beads and white cane to Peter she said that it was at the graveside at the First Baptist Christ Church that Mr. Hawkins had told Mrs. Major Hoffman that the Salvation Army should have all the things in Augustina's house in exchange for the help that they had given the Di Santangelo family with food. Mr. Hawkins told the Mrs. Major Hoffman that he was sure that would be what Miss Augustina would have wanted.

Peter took the cane and the rosary from Willie Hawkins. He touched the crucifix. He fingered the beads, recalling his grandmother sitting out in the back yard near the Shenango River saying the rosary. As he ran his hand over the handle of the white cane he thought about his trips to the Mr. Bump's farm with his grandmother. Of how, now and then, she would rap him gently on the head when he forgot to reply to her prayers with the proper "Amen".

Willie Hawkins went over to the window and stood there watching him and occasionally lifting her bifocals to wipe her eyes.

"It was a terrible day, Sugar," Willie Hawkins said. "I cried all night and Mr. Hawkins refused to come out of his bedroom for supper. And the next morning, before we went to the bus station, Mr. Hawkins sat at the table and kept telling Miss Willie about what drinking will do to a man like Mr. Sam. Mr. Hawkins even made a promise that he would quit going into those white beer gardens if it would make Miss Willie feel better, and Mr. Hawkins not only quit going into the beer gardens, but he took the beer we had in the refrigerator and threw all them bottles away. And Mr. Hawkins never touched any spirits again. And then Mr. Hawkins started to cry, Sugar, and he told Miss Willie that he was going to put his radio and his grasshopper in with the baseball cards in the cigar box for our Sugar. Later, Mr. Hawkins and Miss Willie spent the evening over at the church with the other people in the neighborhood and we prayed to the Almighty God for Miss Augustina's journey to Heaven."

As Willie Hawkins spoke to Peter, he could hear that her voice was trembling.

"Miss Willie," Peter called to her.

When Willie Hawkins started to cry, Peter was visibly moved. The serious expression on his face took on another dimension, one of great concern for Willie Hawkins.

"I'm sorry for crying like this, Sugar. Miss Willie

doesn't mean to upset you."

"I'm not upset, Miss Willie," Peter said as he walked over to Willie Hawkins, who stood by the window, crying. As he put his arms around her he felt how slight and frail she had become in the years since he had known her.

Willie Hawkins continued to speak in a voice that was full of the pain of remembering her friend, Augustina. "I tried to tell Miss Augustina time and time again that something terrible was going to happen with Mr. Sam drinking and hitting Miss Augustina and Sugar like that. But Miss Augustina told this woman how much she loved Mr. Sam."

Peter stood by Willie Hawkins in silence, his arms around her.

"Miss Augustina was like a sister to me, Sugar. I never had a sister, but Miss Augustina made up for it."

Something in what Willie Hawkins said to Peter touched him very deeply. Perhaps it was the knowledge that he had once had a sister who was now lost to him. He hesitated before speaking to her. Then he said, "I know that my mother loved you and Mr. Hawkins very much, Miss Willie."

Then, quietly he asked her, "Will you take me to my mother's grave?"

III

It was bitterly cold as Willie Hawkins and Peter walked toward the cemetery. The winter snowflakes danced around them, then fell soundlessly to the frozen earth. Willie Hawkins remarked that she could not remember a winter day that was so cold as that Saturday, two days before the celebration of the birth of Christ. She pointed to the new First Baptist Christ Church. "It took us years to raise the money for our new church, Sugar," she said as they passed the church. "But we finally got a new church for my Jesus in the neighborhood. And that was way before the housing project people came here to look at the neighborhood.

Do you go to church, Sugar?"

"No, Miss Willie," Peter replied. "I haven't been to church since I married Margaret." He looked at Willie Hawkins and said, "Margaret takes the children with her to church every Sunday and they are enrolled in Bible School. I'm still a little confused about religion, Miss Willie."

"You are not the first person to tell this woman that they are confused about my Jesus, Sugar. But, as Miss Willie told them, Jesus comes to you inside, and when you are ready, Sugar, He will be with you, as He is now, only you're not aware of it right now. But you will, Sugar, when the time comes. You will. You have to read the Gospels for the words of Jesus as He talks about the Father. In Matthew's, Sugar, is the Sermon on the Mount, and it represents everything that my Jesus wants us to do on the good Earth. To this old woman, Sugar, this Sermon is the way we are to live until the Master calls us Home. It is what my Jesus wants us to do. To be humble and to put our trust in God, because the Almighty is the only fate that can give us the strength and the hope to cope with the evils of the earth. You must put your whole trust in God, Sugar. God means everything. Everything, Sugar."

Peter listened gravely to the words of his old friend, Willie Hawkins. He heard and felt the simple good-ness of this woman who spoke to him as they walked together to the graves of his family. He believed quite simply what he believed, for he did not know how to do otherwise. And so he walked straight ahead, without swerving, into the winter winds of New Castle. He knew that he was ready now to confront the deep feelings and the knowledge which would inevitably come to him when, finally, he stood by the graves of his beloved mother and his grandmother.

Peter Di Santangelo knew with absolute certainty that the two women who were buried here represented the first real love he had known on this earth.

As they reached the cemetery, Willie Hawkins pointed to a tall tree whose bare limbs reached out in all directions. "They're buried right next to that tree, Sugar."

As they walked toward the graves, Peter could feel his heart's pace begin to quicken. He did not speak for fear that what he was feeling would tell in his voice and upset Willie Hawkins. Some part of him recalled the little boy who had taken the long trip alone on a bus to Philadelphia. A gust of wind hit him in the face and stung his nose and eyes. As he walked with Willie Hawkins up a slight hill toward the gravesites, his memory flashed to the day so many years ago that Dabney Hawkins and this same Willie Hawkins had held his hand and whisked him, along with his sister, Connie, to the Salvation Army headquarters on that day that 'Satan had walked through their neighborhood'.

The hill which the two of them climbed as they

headed toward the graves was a slight one but for some reason it felt like a mountain to Peter. So many feelings were coming unleashed in him.

Finally, they stopped walking and stood quietly before the two graves which were marked by concrete crosses. Peter looked from one to the other. He stood closest to the grave of his mother.

"I come here every day, Sugar, to pay my respects to Mr. Hawkins, Miss Augustina and the Mrs. Mamo. This is where I was this morning when you were waiting for Miss Willie. But, the Good Lord knows that I have never brought Miss Augustina anything but plastic flowers until this day." Willie Hawkins looked at the grave of Augustina Di Santangelo and knelt down near the front of the grave. "Miss Augustina?" she whispered. "I hate to bother you again after talking to you this morning, but I brought our Sugar with me this time to see my Miss Augustina and the Mrs. Mamo. Yes, oh Glory Jesus! That is what I said, Miss Augustina, Sugar! Now I am going to leave the two of you alone but I will be back first thing tomorrow morning to talk to you, Miss Augustina."

Peter put his hands around Willie Hawkins and helped her to stand. She brushed the lower part of her dress to remove the snow. "Thank you, Sugar," she said to Peter. "I always say hello to the Mrs. Mamo, too, Sugar, but I have to say it to Miss Augustina because the Mrs. Mamo never spoke English. Now Miss Willie will just leave you here with Miss Augustina while Miss Willie goes up and talks to Mr. Hawkins for a spell." She turned, then, and walked away from Peter.

Peter watched Willie Hawkins as she walked on up the hill to the top where she knelt at the back of Dabney Hawkins' grave. Then slowly he turned back to his mother and grandmother's graves. He thought that perhaps he should have the remains moved to Buffalo, but then thought about their friends, Dabney Hawkins and Mr. Tom, and eventually Willie Hawkins coming here to rest, and he realized that his mother and his grandmother did not belong in Buffalo, but here, in the First Baptist Christ Church Cemetery, with the people who had taken care of them and had loved both of them so much. He knelt down to pray.

"Hello, Mother," he spoke in a solemn tone. "I guess you and Mamo realize how much I have missed both of you. I used to go to the window at the orphanage every morning before mass and look out the window, hoping to see you coming for me, Mother. And then I guess you remember when I stopped going to the window.

"As a child, I didn't quite understand why you never came to the orphanage, and I thought that perhaps you were mad at me for going over to the house to get the cigar box that afternoon, and that if I had not gone over to the house, we would still be together. But, as I grew older, I realized that what happened would have

happened, eventually, but under different circumstances. You will just have to forgive me for not mentioning to any of the other children at the orphanage
about what had happened to my family when they
asked, but I was so frightened because I had disobeyed
you. And to this day I have never even mentioned anything about our family to Margaret for fear of losing
her, although I should know better. I know that I will
tell her at the right time, Mother.

"I think that you know I have been a good husband
to Margaret, and I have been a good father to our three
children. They are all that I have, and, at times I think
they are the only thing that keeps me going. And when
I look at them I think so many times of you, Mamo
and Sister, and of how unfortunate it is that my children did not have a chance to know you, and to be
touched by your tender love.

"I wish they could see how beautiful you were. I
can still recall you by the wringer-washer, smiling and
talking to me. And Mamo, with her beautiful, beautiful white hair. God, how I miss both of you, dear
Mother. My heart is so broken that I never sing to the
earth anymore.

"If I had any idea where I could find Sister, you
know that I would go and get Sister and take care of
her. But I honestly feel that Sister sings with you and
Mamo, Mother. And if she is not with you, I know that
you both watch over her every day, as you do for me

and for my family. And that is about all that I can hope for, Mother. To know that you and Mamo will look out for my children, and to give me the guidance to do what is right for my family, and to watch my children live in peace."

Peter sighed as he said the word, "peace". The innocent look on his face as he spoke these words so tenderly to his mother was that of a boy. There was so much in him that was unfinished, so many unspoken words.

He continued to speak aloud to his mother. "I do pray for both of you every night, and I know deep inside of me that I am so very proud of you and Mamo. And I know that you dwell in Heaven with Mamo, Sister, and with Mr. Hawkins. I love all of you so much, Mother.

"I will leave you now, Mother, and pay my respect to Mr. Hawkins and Mr. Tom. I am sorry things turned out the way they did for our family. I do know that we have to put our lives in the hands of the *Spiritual God* and respect how the *Spiritual God* handles our lives. Good-bye my dear, dear, beloved mother."

Peter stood and walked to the stark and erect cement crosses on that winter's day. He bent down and kissed them and as he did so, he felt a certain peace. Still carrying his grandmother's white cane and his mother's rosary beads, he went up to the crest of the hill to join Willie Hawkins and to pray at the grave sites of Dabney Hawkins and Mr. Tom.

When they left the cemetery, Peter mentioned to Willie Hawkins that when he arrived at the orphanage back in 1947, the officials had taken away the school box and the cigar box which the Hawkins family had given to Peter, so that he did not have anything with him to remind him of New Castle while he was at the orphanage.

Willie Hawkins insisted that she walk with Peter over the viaduct and to the car. Peter objected, mentioning the cold, but Willie Hawkins ignored him and walked at his side through the neighborhood, over the viaduct, and to the car. As Peter prepared himself to leave Miss Willie, he steeled himself against the emotion he was feeling and forced his voice to remain calm. He took both of her hands in his which made the old woman look even smaller than she was. "Miss Willie," said Peter. "I shall never forget this day. You cannot know how much it means to me to have been with you and to have visited the graves of my family. I'll come again to see you, Miss Willie," Peter promised.

Willie Hawkins shook her head. "No, Sugar. You do not belong here anymore. This is a bad place for you. There is nothing here but this old, ugly nightmare that happened a long, long time ago." She moved closer to Peter. "There is no sense in coming back to see Miss Willie again, Sugar. I see Mr. Hawkins and Miss Augustina more clearly every night when I bed myself. I don't have too much time, Sugar, until the Lord's angels come for Miss Willie in His golden chariot, and take Miss Willie to Paradise. I told Miss Augustina a long time ago that I only live for the day I see the Almighty God, and talk to Jesus and walk in Paradise. You have a woman and children of your own, Sugar. Miss Margaret is your family. And please, Sugar. Please don't ever be ashamed of where you came from and how you lived here in the old neighborhood. It is against the Lord to try to be something that you're not, or to be ashamed of the way the Lord made you. You tell your children what a fine, fine woman Miss Augustina was, and that there is no one who comes to the Lord's earth any better than Miss Augustina. No one is any better than you, Sugar, on the Lord's earth. And you, Sugar, are no better than anyone else on the Lord's earth. You must not forget that. Never." She tried to smile, as she continued talking. "You tell Miss Margaret and the children all about us, Sugar."

Peter embraced Miss Willie and then kissed her. "Oh, Miss Willie," he whispered, "I have been so confused."

"I know, Sugar. It is the Lord's way of testing us."

"Who is going to take care of you, Miss Willie?" Peter asked, still embracing Willie Hawkins. "You are all alone and by yourself."

"You should know better than to ask Miss Willie such a question, Sugar," she replied, as she stepped back and looked at him. "Jesus takes care of me, and when you have Jesus, you are never lonely, Sugar," she said.

She smiled slightly as she said these words, tearfully, to Peter. Something in her smile reassured him that she was, indeed, not alone and that she would be alright. Miss Willie's kindness was what Peter remembered most about her from when he was a little boy, and today as he was having trouble leaving her, it was the warm kindness which showed through her tearful smile which would help Peter to go on his way.

His mind flashed back just for a moment to that "other" day when he was six and Miss Willie and Mr. Dabney Hawkins had sent him on his way to Philadelphia on the bus. He wondered if it was possible that he was only able to make that long, solitary journey because of Willie Hawkins and Mr. Dabney Hawkins being there with him when he left.

The snow continued to fall. Willie Hawkins, ignoring the snowfall, opened her large, black purse and removed from it her Bible.

"I have had this Good Book for a very long time, Sugar. It belonged to my mother, Mrs. Hawkins. I have read and reread this Good Book and now I am ready to go home to my God."

Willie Hawkins did not open the Bible. The slight old woman dressed all in black stood quite close to Peter and looked firmly into his hazel-green eyes. He stood there, unmoving, in a dark, navy overcoat, collar up against the cold, his stick straight hair, darker than ever against its' snowy background and listened earnestly as Willie Hawkins recited from the Book of Ecclesiastes:

> *"To every thing there is a season,*
> *and a time to every purpose under the*
> *Heaven:*
> *A time to be born, and a time to die;*
> *A time to plant, and a time to pluck up*
> *that which is planted;*
> *A time to kill, and a time to heal,*
> *A time to break down, and a time to*
> *build up;*
> *A time to weep and a time to laugh;*
> *A time to mourn, and a time to dance;*
> *A time to cast away stones, and a time*
> *to gather stones together;*
> *A time to embrace and a time to refrain*
> *from embracing;*
> *A time to get, and a time to lose;*
> *A time to keep, and a time to cast away;*
> *A time to rend, and a time to sew;*
> *A time to keep silence, and a time*
> *to speak;*
> *A time to love, and a time to hate;*
> *A time of war, and a time of peace."*

Willie Hawkins handed the Bible to Peter. "I want you to have this, Sugar. I want you to read the Bible to your children. Feed them from the Testaments, Sugar, and watch your children grow in joy."

"Thank you, Miss Willie," Peter said, taking the Bible from Willie Hawkins. "Margaret reads the Bible to our children. And I will tell them all about my family, and about you, Miss Willie, and Mr. Hawkins."

"I have to go now, Sugar. I am tired."

"I'll drive you back to your unit, Miss Willie."

"No, thank you, Sugar. There is no need for you ever to cross the viaduct again. That is a thing of the past. And don't worry about Miss Willie, because Miss Willie is in good hands. Good-bye, Sugar. Thank you for coming to see Miss Willie. God be with you, Sugar."

"Please let me drive you back, Miss Willie? It's too cold for you to go over the viaduct with the snow and the wind blowing like this. Please?"

Willie Hawkins did not say another word. She shook her head, turned away, and headed for the viaduct.

"Miss Willie!" shouted Peter.

Again a memory from that "other" day flashed painfully into Peter's mind. He saw himself as a little boy, hanging out of a bus window, calling to Miss Willie. But, on this day the grown-up Peter, unlike the little Peter of long ago, knew that he could not cling to Willie Hawkins and to New Castle, Pennsylvania.

In spite of the terrible, wrenching pain in Peter's heart, in spite of words that could barely come, so choked was he with the emotion of letting go, finally, of a family that almost never was, Peter shouted out again.

"Miss Willie! I love you, Miss Willie!"

· Peter stood for several minutes, watching Willie Hawkins trudge courageously over the viaduct. He watched as now and then a sharp, gust of wind blew harshly against her fragile body. He watched as she walked straight ahead, never for a moment losing her sense of balance or of where she was going. He watched as she did not look back. He watched as, eventually, her dear, slight figure disappeared into the "neighborhood".

Another sharp pain grabbed at Peter's chest and he knew, instantly, in his mind and in his soul that Willie Hawkins, Peter's one connection on earth with his beloved mother, his grandmother and his sister had now gone, physically, from his life.

IV

Peter drove out of the parking lot of the hardware discount store and left the city of New Castle, heading for Interstate 79 North. When he came to the end of the Interstate, he did not go into the city of Erie to pick up the Simmons Wire-Rope and Container Corporation contract as he had planned. Instead, he took Interstate 90 East toward the New York state line, and into the city of Buffalo.

Large, dense snowflakes poured out of the sky as Peter drove into the driveway, got out of his car and ran toward the house. "Margaret! Margaret!" he called as he ran.

Margaret came out of the house and onto the walkway. When Peter reached her, he called her name again, put his arms around her, and kissed her.

"Peter! What's the matter?" Margaret exclaimed, looking at the white cane, rosary beads, and Willie Hawkin's Bible which Peter held. "What happened, Peter?"

"Nothing happened, honey," Peter answered. "I'm just so glad to be home. To be with you and the children." He saw that Margaret was staring at the objects in his hands. "It's a long story, Margaret. A very long story. I have something very important to tell you while we put up the Christmas tree and wrap the children's presents."

Peter put his arms around Margaret again as they walked toward the front porch. As he glanced in through the picture window, he saw that Margaret and the children had already started to decorate the Christmas tree, and the bright, colored lights around the front window reflected beautifully on the heavy white snow.

As Peter's eyes became moist, he stopped and turned Margaret toward him. "I love you so very much, Margaret. Only God knows how much I love you, and how much I need you." And Peter realized at that moment that although he and Margaret would be able to give their children all of the love they had and everything that they would ever need in life, the greatest thing he could do for his children was to love their mother Margaret in the eyes of their children.

"Peter," Margaret said. "You are starting to worry me. What happened to you today?"

"I met an old family friend whom I haven't seen for a very long time. I'll tell you all about it later. I just want you to know how much I love you and how much I love our children." Peter elevated his head and directed his eyes toward the sky, vigilant of the graceful snowflakes coming down. As he lowered his head he looked at Margaret and he tried to smile as he embraced his beloved wife.

Later that night, in bed, Peter disclosed to Margaret the story of his family. Margaret held Peter against her as he cried, drenching her with his words.

She listened, but she did not cry, not that she did not want to, as he spoke to her about growing up in New Castle, Pennsylvania.

She listened, every now and then kissing Peter's forehead, as he cried out, achingly, chockingly, speaking of his mother, his grandmother and his sister Connie.

She listened, resisting the tears, as she braced her husband. She stroked his hair with her left hand and fingers, as he spoke of Willie Hawkins and her father Dabney Hawkins, and the time, oh, so long ago, when they frighteningly and lightningly ran the risk and rushed into the heart of white New Castle to save Peter and Connie from their father.

She listened, looking straight ahead of her at the

nightlight on the wall of the bedroom, holding Peter as tight as she could, as he uncontrollably sobbed, telling her about the death of his grandmother, the death of his mother, and the separation from his sister Connie.

Margaret listened, kissing Peter's tears, as he spoke of his unexpected, unexplainable, but increasingly important trip to New Castle to find his childhood, Willie Hawkins, and of their journey to the cemetery to visit his mother and grandmother's graves.

In time, Peter, exhausted, fell asleep in Margaret's arms. She sat in bed holding Peter, hearing his words repeated in her heart. As Peter eventually moved his head from Margaret's arms to his pillow, Margaret gently got out of bed and walked out of the bedroom, through the hallway, descended the stairs and entered the living room.

As she settled down on one of the sofas, Cooper springed onto the sofa and looked at his owner. Margaret put her arms around the golden retriever and held him. She buried her face into the dog's winter hair on his head and neck, clinging and hugging Cooper. When she could no longer govern her pain, she started to cry as she held on to Cooper. The gentle dog did not move, but rested his head on Margaret's shoulder as she trembled and cried from listening to her husband's broken heart.

V

On Christmas morning, Peter and his family exchanged their holiday gifts with each other. The day before, the family had picked up Margaret's parents, Michael and Eleanor Michalojko at the Buffalo International Airport.

While Margaret and her mother Eleanor worked in the kitchen preparing the holiday dinner, Peter sat with his father-in-law. As Michael Michalojko spoke of the ranch and Tessie and her son Montana, Peter looked at this man who meant so much to him. He wondered to himself how it could have been possible as a child to have had Dabney Hawkins as a surrogate father, and for the past 18 years, this man sitting across from him as his father.

Like Dabney Hawkins, there was a warmhearted-ness that came with the quiet strength of Michael Michalojko. The gracious and gratifying, gentleness of his eyes, the distinguished warm smile that only hon-est, good people express on their face. A man whom Peter understood, learned to love, and learned to re-spect by vigilantly witnessing the interaction between Michael and Eleanor over the years. He witnessed the gentle love they showed for one another, the softness in their voices as they spoke to each other, the love in their eyes when they looked at each other.

At the orphanage Peter had always wondered why the 5th Commandment read *Honor Thy Father And Thy Mother,* and not Love Thy Father And Mother. Yet, it was through Michael and Eleanor Michalojko that Peter understood the *Honor.* Peter knew that he would only know one woman in his lifetime, Margaret. He loved her with a passion that, at times, overwhelmed him by the joy, the happiness, the love she unconditionally gave to Peter. And in looking at her father sitting across from him, Peter knew that he owed all of this joy, happiness and love to Michael and Eleanor Michalojko, for one night, many years ago, their love for each other con-ceived a child. A child that was now the stable founda-tion of strength in Peter's life.

Peter kept looking and listening to this good man

he so honored sitting in front of him talking. He also thought of another man and woman during his child-hood that he would immortally honor and perpetually love. Dabney and Willie Hawkins.

Before dinner, Peter walked into Margaret's studio. He looked at the grand piano that her parents had given to her when she graduated from Juilliard, and at the wooden chairs in the room where Margaret's students, of all ages, came for their piano lessons. He walked over to her desk and picked up the telephone and with the help of the operator was given Willie Hawkins' number. He dialed the number and Miss Willie answered the phone. They wished each other a Merry Christmas. Willie Hawkins mentioned that she had spent most of the morning at the church with Miss Libby, and that Miss Libby was helping Miss Willie in the kitchen preparing their holiday dinner.

Miss Willie asked about Peter's family. Peter answered, and then asked Willie Hawkins to stay on the line while he went to get Margaret. As Margaret entered the studio she picked up the telephone and started to speak to Willie Hawkins. Peter walked out of the room, gently closing the door behind him, so that Margaret and Willie Hawkins would be alone during their conversation. In time, Margaret, her eyes moist, came out of the studio and walked over to Peter and hugged him.

As they sat down for dinner, Peter looked at his

wife, his children, and his in-laws as they humbly lowered their heads in prayer. He watched and listened as
his mother-in-law Eleanor said the prayer of thanks,
and he thought of Dabney Hawkins at the kitchen table
so many years ago. He looked at his father-in-law
Michael, his head bent in grace, his hand in Eleanor's
hand. Peter's eyes dampened as he looked at them and
understood how much he loved them. He turned his
head and looked at Margaret, his heart full of love for
her. He turned and looked at his children Cathy, Teresa
and Anthony, their heads bowed in silence as they listened to their grandmother. His eyes teared up for a
few seconds.

As they ate dinner, Peter looked at his children. It
was time to tell them of his family. As they grew older,
he would tell them the whole story, but for now, he
knew what to say to them. He smiled and began to
speak. "I'm going to tell you about your other grandmother, my mother Augustina, whom you never met."

Margaret reached over and put her hand in Peter's
hand as he spoke.

"When your father was born, I lived in a small town
called New Castle, which is in the western part of Pennsylvania. I lived with my mother, your grandmother. Her
name was Augustina. I also had a sister, your aunt. Her
name was Connie. My grandmother also lived with us.
She was sightless, blind, and we called your great-grand-
mother Mamo." Peter looked at Margaret and smiled.

He again turned to his children. "Unfortunately, I don't have any pictures to show you of my family, but we were very poor, and in those days we couldn't afford a camera. We lived next door to a woman whose name was Willie Hawkins, who taught me my alphabet and how to count my numbers. Her father lived with her and his name was Dabney Hawkins and he had a pet grasshopper that he called Smitty. Well, Miss Willie Hawkins really loved your grandmother's spaghetti, and after work, Mr. Hawkins and his daughter Miss Willie would come over to our house for supper......."

*   *   *   *   *   *   *

On Sunday, April 15, 1979, Peter telephoned Willie Hawkins from Michael and Eleanor Michalojko's ranch in Wyoming to wish her a Happy Easter. The telephone call was answered by Miss Libby who told Peter that Miss Libby had come over to Miss Willie's for coffee and that they were supposed to go over to the church. Miss Willie did not answer the door, so Miss Libby used her key to enter Miss Willie's unit. She found Miss Willie lying in bed, dead. Miss Libby cried as she spoke to Peter. She told him that she did not know what she was going to do, because Miss Willie had been her best friend and family. She told Peter that she would go into the bedroom and tell Miss Willie that her Sugar telephoned to wish her a Happy Easter.

Margaret stood by the telephone hoping to speak to Willie Hawkins, but she noticed Peter's silence as he listened. Peter put the receiver down as he looked at Margaret. He put his arms around her. "Miss Willie died sometime during the night," he spoke in a whisper as he held Margaret. "Miss Willie is home, Margaret. She is looking at her God, talking to her Jesus and walking in Paradise. Miss Willie is finally home."

And in Margaret's arms, Peter Di Santangelo, his eyes moist, smiled, for he knew that he had finally crossed the Shenango River and had gone beyond the viaduct.

P E A C E

"The woman was made out of a rib
out of the side of Adam; not of
his feet to be trampled on by him,
but out of his side to be equal with
him, under his arms to be protected
and, near his heart to be loved."

—*Matthew Henry 1725*

William Carnuche received his M.Ed. graduate degree in the Department of Psychology in Education at the University of Pittsburgh and continues his advanced training at the post-master's level. As a courtesy graduate student at Catholic University of America, Washington, D.C., he completed his supervised practicum and internship as a psychotherapist in the State of Maryland Penal System in a coordinated field experience between Catholic University of America and the University of Pittsburgh. He is certified by the Commonwealth of Pennsylvania as a secondary school counselor and is a psychotherapist in private practice. He is a member of the American Counseling Association, American Mental Health Counselors Association and founder of Pittsburgh Counseling Associates, Inc.